PUFFIN BOOKS

INTO THE FOURTH AT TREBIZON

When Rebecca and Tish arrive at Trebizon School for the beginning of their year in the Fourth, they have a mad scramble to bag two adjoining rooms on the second floor of Court House. For the six friends are determined to stay together. But their plans are foiled when Ingrid Larsson, a beautiful new girl from Sweden, is foisted upon them. To her dismay, Mara has to move into a single room.

Rebecca is charged with showing Ingrid the ropes and it is soon clear that Ingrid is going to cast a chill over Rebecca's term. Just to begin with, she finds she has to take Ingrid ice-skating instead of going to watch Tish's brother Robbie, who is at nearby Garth College, play rugby as she had promised.

Meanwhile, Tish, who is favourite in the election for the position of Fourth Year Head of Games, has been making secret advance plans for the national seven-a-side hockey competition for which Trebizon has been entered. But suddenly and unaccountably opinion turns against Tish, and there is uproar when her plans are mysteriously leaked. Who can be behind it all?

Mystery and intrigue abound in this eighth story in the fantastically popular Trebizon series.

Anne Digby was born in Kingston-upon-Thames, Surrey, but has lived in the West Country for many years. As well as the Trebizon books, she is the author of the popular *Me, Jill Robinson* stories.

THE **TREBIZON** BOOKS (in reading order)

ANNE DIGBY

INTO THE FOURTH AT
TREBIZON

PUFFIN BOOKS

PUFFIN BOOKS

Published by the Penguin Group
27 Wrights Lane, London W 8 5 T Z, England
Viking Penguin Inc., 40 West 23rd Street, New York, New York 10010, USA
Penguin Books Australia Ltd, Ringwood, Victoria, Australia
Penguin Books Canada Ltd, 2801 John Street, Markham, Ontario, Canada L 3 R 1 B 4
Penguin Books (NZ) Ltd, 182–190 Wairau Road, Auckland 10, New Zealand

Penguin Books Ltd, Registered Offices: Harmondsworth, Middlesex, England

First published by Granada Publishing 1982
Published in Puffin Books 1988

Made and printed in Great Britain by
Cox and Wyman Ltd, Reading, Berks
Filmset in Linotron Ehrhardt by
Rowland Phototypesetting Ltd,
Bury St Edmunds, Suffolk

To Francis

CONTENTS

ONE

EXCITING PLANS

When Rebecca Mason went into the Fourth at Trebizon, there were difficulties. They had nothing to do with school work, because her timetable was settled now and she knew which subjects she would be taking for GCSE. Rather it was to do with the friendships in her life, and especially with the arrival at Court House of a girl called Ingrid Larsson.

It was surprising that a girl as cool and peaceful looking as Ingrid could create dissension. She was quite beautiful, in fact.

'In an *icy* sort of way,' Tish Anderson was to comment. 'The Ice Queen herself.'

'Oh, Tish, what a strange description!' Rebecca had laughed. 'You're just jealous!'

It wasn't until much later, in December, that Rebecca remembered the description. That was when the frost and ice came – real ice – freezing all the little lakes and streams around Trebizon, thick enough to skate on. And that was when Ingrid, in her high white skating boots and flowing cloak, took command of her territory. Rebecca remembered then what Tish had said and thought about it deeply.

Nothing could have been less icy than the day they returned to school.

It was a warm September day. In fact it was very stuffy in the supermini, driving all the way from London. It had been cool enough when they'd left, in the very early morning, but by the time they got to the west country the sun was high.

'I wonder what it's going to be like in the Fourth?' said Rebecca.

'You'll soon know,' said Robbie Anderson, who was Tish's older brother. He and Rebecca were sitting together in the back of the car. 'I wish you'd let me drive, Helen.'

'Don't be silly, Robbie.'

Helen Anderson, who was driving, was Tish and Robbie's elder sister. Her new car was small and fast and much more reliable than her previous one. Tish was keeping her company in the front seat and plying her with questions. Helen worked in London and had been getting into some interesting situations lately. Robbie and Rebecca liked being in the back together and on the way down they'd exchanged photos, something they'd promised each other during the course of a long phone conversation the previous weekend.

'As long as we're first to Court House, I don't care what it's like in the Fourth or who drives!' laughed Tish, staring at the road ahead. 'I'll die if we don't get the rooms we want!'

'It's going to be complicated if we don't,' agreed Rebecca.

'The suspense is killing me,' grunted Robbie, who had already heard several variations on this theme. He said to Tish – 'You'd better get them, after all this. I could have had a lie-in. I don't have any rooms to bag. I'll just be given a sordid little cubicle like everyone else in the Lower Sixth.'

'Oh, Robbie, they're not as bad as all that!' protested Helen. 'There's a bed and a desk and somewhere to stick posters, and a place to plug in an electric kettle. Of course, when you get in the Upper Sixth, you get a proper room –'

'How do you know?' grinned Tish.

'Oh,' Helen concentrated on the road ahead, and smiled. She'd been at Trebizon herself some years previously and had had friends at Garth College, where Robbie was now. 'I just know, that's all.'

'I'm not complaining, anyway,' said Robbie. 'A cube suits me fine. I'm just glad I haven't got to go through a lot of hassle over new rooms, like you two.'

It was because of the new rooms that they'd grabbed the chance to come really early by road, instead of by the usual train. Doctor and Mrs Anderson had left for the States and Rebecca's parents were flying back to Saudi Arabia that day, now their London leave was over. Helen had offered to drive these three down to the west country, because she wanted to see some old friends who lived near Trebizon and stay the night with them.

So the Andersons had driven down from Hertfordshire via the M25 to South London to pick Rebecca up, eaten a delicious breakfast of sizzling bacon and eggs cooked for them by Mrs Mason, and then whisked away Rebecca, her trunk and her tennis rackets.

'Write to us, Becky! Tell us all your news!'

'Of course I will! 'Bye, Mum! 'Bye, Dad! You make sure you write to me!'

That was her last glimpse of them, standing on the front doorstep of the terraced house. It would soon be let to strangers again and it would be next summer before the three of them were together again there, for a few happy weeks.

The car was now less than three miles from Trebizon.

'There's the turning to Garth, look!' said Robbie. 'Just

dump me off at the gates with my stuff. I don't want to hold you up.'

Helen forked left down the narrow road that led to the boys' school.

Robbie turned to Rebecca and put an arm round her shoulders. He was looking solemn, although his eyes were mischievous.

'How many times have I come and cheered you this summer?'

'Let me see,' said Rebecca, equally solemn and counting on her fingers. Her parents had taken her to several tennis competitions and she'd done remarkably well. 'At least four –'

'Well you've got to come and cheer *me*, now I'm in the team.' He was talking about rugby, of course; always a big thing with Robbie in the winter. 'Okay?'

'Are you really in the First XV?' asked Helen, impressed. She pulled up outside the gates of Garth College. It had one of the best schools' rugby teams in the country. 'Is that definite?'

'Definite,' nodded Robbie.

'Of course it's definite,' said Tish. 'That's why he wouldn't come down early for the Trebizon Open this year.' She was referring to a local mixed doubles tennis tournament, that took place annually on the Trebizon School courts at the end of the summer holidays, just before the tennis nets came down and the netball posts went up. 'He and Rebecca could have partnered each other this year, and I'd have known who to cheer for – not like last year – and they'd have won, too! *And* we could have been back at school yesterday and bagged the rooms, instead of having to rush.' Tish shrugged, then grinned. 'Saving himself for rugby.'

'I had to do weight training, Tish. We've got our first match on Saturday!'

'Shouldn't be so weak and floppy in the first place.'

'Stop arguing, you two,' said Rebecca. 'I hadn't specially wanted to enter, anyway.'

That wasn't quite true. Rebecca really meant that she hadn't wanted to enter with anybody else, if she couldn't enter with Robbie.

He was getting out of the car now, to get his trunk off the roof rack. He unroped it and then lifted it down effortlessly. Helen reversed the car outside the college gates, ready to leave. Robbie opened the back door and ducked his head in.

'Okay, Rebeck? Come and watch the match on Saturday?'

'All right then,' said Rebecca.

They drove away, towards the town. In the High Street there was still a fair sprinkling of holiday-makers, pushing push-chairs, eating ice-creams and carrying buckets and spades. As soon as they were out of town, whipping along the top road and gazing at the blue waters of Trebizon Bay, Tish said:

'Nearly there.'

'Mmm,' said Rebecca.

'Rebecca –'

'Mmmm?'

'When's tennis training this term?'

'Sunday fortnights, I think.'

'I know he's my brother, but you're not going to be a paid-up member of the Garth College supporters' club every Saturday, are you? Shivering on the touch-line in all weathers . . .'

'No fear!' laughed Rebecca. 'But I'd like to go and watch him a few times maybe.'

'Good,' said Tish. 'You see,' she added mysteriously, 'I've got *other* plans for you. If –'

'Really?' Rebecca was intrigued. 'What plans?'

'At last!' exclaimed Helen. She turned the car in through the school's wrought iron gates. The wooded school drive lay ahead. 'We're here. I'll drive you two to Court House and dump you if you don't mind. I'll just have time to go and say "hello" to Miss Welbeck and then I must get to Katy and John's. They've got a meal waiting for me!'

As the car bumped slowly through the school grounds, observing the strict speed limit, Rebecca leaned forward and questioned Tish some more.

'What plans? What are the plans to do with?'

'Hockey!'

Helen glanced at her younger sister in amusement.

'You mean to say Tish hasn't told you about her plans yet? She's been organizing it all through the holidays, pieces of paper everywhere. There's some sort of master plan cooked up, I think.'

'But I'd never make the Third Team!' exclaimed Rebecca. 'There are others better than me.'

Now that they were older, if Tish were elected head of games this year she'd be given the job of helping to choose the school's Third Eleven. Being exceptionally good at hockey she already played for the Second Eleven herself, with senior girls, and might even get into the First Eleven quite soon.

'It's nothing to do with the Third Eleven,' said Tish, rather abruptly. She seemed embarrassed by Helen's mention of all those pieces of paper. 'Or elevens at all,' she added, in a mutter.

'Much more exciting!' said Helen.

'Well, what's the matter, Tish?' asked Rebecca. 'Why haven't I heard about this?'

They were passing within sight of Tavistock House, one of the other middle school boarding houses. It lay this side of south tennis courts, not very far from the main school building. Tish seemed to glance that way.

'I didn't mean to let anything out yet,' she said, still looking slightly uncomfortable. 'I mean I haven't actually been *made* head of games yet. I was going to say I've got some plans, *if* I am. Now Helen's made it sound as if I just take it for granted –'

'Oh, Tish!' Rebecca laughed. 'What does it matter, just between us? Who ever's going to bother to stand against you anyway –'

Then Rebecca realized why Tish had glanced towards the rival House.

'Laura Wilkins?'

'We did have a bit of a fight with Tavistock last term, getting Aba in against Laura like that by seven votes!' said Tish wryly. 'They've probably got it in for us now!'

'I don't think Laura will want to stand against you, Tish!' smiled Rebecca. 'And even if she does, you'll beat her by – well, by seventy votes I should think!'

'Do you really think so?' Tish cheered up.

'So come on!' said Rebecca. 'Tell me what this master plan is all about –'

The car scrunched over gravel and came to a halt.

'It's Court! We're here!' squealed Tish.

'I thought you hadn't noticed,' said Helen. 'Go and see about the rooms. I'll wait here with your stuff –'

The two friends almost fell out of the car and hurtled towards the front door.

'Nobody here yet!' cried Tish. 'I only hope we're in time –'

The master plan would have to wait.

TWO

GETTING THE ROOMS

When Rebecca and her friends, known as 'the six', had first entered Court House (exactly a year before), the rooms had been just right. Previously as juniors they'd been in dormitories, over at Juniper House, but promotion to the middle school and being allocated to Court had meant sharing study bedrooms for the first time.

As Third Years, they had had to come into Court on the ground floor, where all the rooms were three-bedders. It had worked perfectly. They'd had two adjacent rooms, Rebecca and Tish and their great friend Sue Murdoch in one: Mara Leonodis, Margot Lawrence and Sally (Elf) Elphinstone in the room next door.

Now, as Fourth Years, they were going up in the world – litcrally – to the first floor of the boarding house. At first they'd bccn disappointed to think that there were no three-bedders on the first floor, just a motley collection of twos and singles, and one four-bedder. They'd never be in threes again! Next year, in the Fifth, everyone had cubicles on the top floor, to get plenty of peace and quiet for private study.

But during the summer holidays Tish had done some

research. She'd rung Sarah Turner, who'd been a Fourth last year, and got the exact layout. Then she'd phoned her friends.

'There are two singles,' she had told Rebecca. 'One of them's horrible, right along the corridor and round the corner, stuck on its own. Margaret Exton had it, she thought it was a great arrangement.'

'I expect everyone else did, too,' laughed Rebecca. 'Okay, let's forget that one.'

'The other single's all right, it inter-connects with a two-bedder. It would suit us three fine, but there wouldn't be anything to suit the other three. So there's only one answer and it's perfect, even better than we had downstairs.'

'What's that?' asked Rebecca hopefully.

'The four-bedder. You see, it inter-connects with a two-bedder. So the six of us can still be together – more together, in fact! And it's at the back – you know how we like being at the back!'

'Terrific!' Rebecca exclaimed. Then she asked, 'Who'd go where?'

'Mara wants to be with us. I've had a letter from her.'

'That's right, she said so. After camp. How would Elf and Margot feel?'

'Oh, those two will definitely want to share. They can have the two-bedder, us four can have the big room – it's perfect, Rebeck!'

Afterwards, Rebecca had remembered something and rung Tish back.

'What does Sue think?'

Tish was silent for a moment.

'Oh, you know Sue. She liked everything just as it was.'

So Rebecca had decided to ring Sue herself.

'It's just my scraping my violin, Rebecca. You two are used to it. You don't even notice if I can't cope with something –'

Sue was a Trebizon music scholar and in the orchestra. Although the school had its own music centre and Sue spent a lot of time there, she often practised in the room as well, if she had something difficult on hand.

'But Mara loves music –'

'That's the trouble. You know Mara, she's got perfect pitch. I'm a bit worried it'll get on her nerves!'

'Oh, Sue, don't!' Rebecca had laughed out loud, with a sudden feeling of relief. 'Is that all? I thought it was something serious.'

Everything was going to be fine. As long as they could get those rooms. They'd have to make sure they did!

Rebecca and Tish took the stairs two at a time.

'There *is* someone here!' Tish whispered in horror. 'I can hear them moving around!'

'Oh, no,' said Rebecca. 'Don't say we're too late –'

They were on the first floor of Court House now, looking along the main landing where most of the rooms lay. Doors were open. A trunk was in one doorway, its contents spilling out. There was the sound of voices now and someone had turned a radio on.

'Come on,' said Tish, biting her lip.

They walked slowly along the landing, looking in through the open doors.

They reached the doorway where the trunk was wedged. Rebecca glanced quickly into the room.

'Oh, *no*! This is it – the four-bedder!'

'It looks as though it's gone!' groaned Tish.

Then, back along the landing, another door burst open

17

and Elizabeth Kendall came out, holding her radio. Jenny Brook-Hayes was just behind her.

'Tish! Rebecca!'

They swung round.

'Whose is this trunk?' wailed Tish.

'Oh, sorry, it's mine,' said Elizabeth. 'We were going to bag that room, but we've found a much better one. A two-bedder – with its own wash basin. Come and see –'

'You mean, this one's still free?' whooped Rebecca.

What a relief!

The other two came down and helped Rebecca and Tish get their luggage off the roof rack. Helen was anxious to drive over to the principal's house and say 'hello'. Miss Welbeck loved seeing old girls and hearing all their news.

'And then I really *must* get to Katy and John's. So all the drama's been worthwhile and you two have got what you wanted!'

'Thanks, Helen!'

'Bye!'

'See you at Christmas!'

The four girls humped the luggage upstairs and then Tish and Rebecca took possession of their prize, the two inter-communicating rooms, strewing belongings on each of the six beds, so that there could be no mistake about it.

'They're small but they're both lovely rooms!' said Rebecca, throwing up one of the two sash windows in the four-bedder and leaning out. It was, as Tish had said, better at the back. There was a big courtyard and some rough grass where Mrs Barrington's hens clucked and a white nanny goat was tethered; and you could see straight across to Norris House, which had once been the stable block to the main house, but was now converted into another middle school boarding house. The rest of Four Alpha lived there, those whose surnames came in the second half of the alphabet, together with some of the Four Betas. 'The way Margot and Elf's room just leads off ours – it's perfect! And I'm glad we're going to have Mara in with us this year.'

'So am I,' said Tish.

They were both very fond of the Greek girl.

'Hey, where's Jane?' she asked suddenly.

'That's a thought,' said Rebecca. 'Perhaps those three don't want to share any more.'

Jane Bowen had shared with Jenny and Elizabeth all last year. Originally she and Mara Leonodis had been in the Beta stream at Trebizon, but at the beginning of the Third Year they'd both been promoted to Three Alpha.

'Oh, haven't you heard?' said Jenny, when they went and asked. 'You remember Jane didn't do too well in the summer exams? Well, she's been put back with the Betas. She's going into Four Beta.'

Rebecca and Tish exchanged startled glances for a moment, thinking of Mara. But then they remembered that Mara had done well in the exams – of course she had!

'So Jane won't be in our form any more?' said Rebecca. 'But –'

'She's changing houses too. Her parents didn't want her to be the only Beta in Court and she's got three really good friends in Norris – you know, Helena and Susan and Mary – they all started in One Beta together. Well there's a spare bed over at Norris, quite apart from Joss's. So she's got a transfer.'

Josselyn Vining was in Rebecca's form and was the most brilliant all-round athlete in memory at Trebizon. She was spending a year at a school in California, having special tennis training, and wouldn't be coming back to Trebizon until the summer term. Rebecca missed her.

'It's better really,' Jenny was saying, still speaking about Jane. 'She's quite relieved about it. She did have a struggle keeping up.'

'Her going will leave a spare place in Court,' said Tish, with interest.

'There's a new girl coming,' Elizabeth informed her.

'Really?'

'What's her name?'

They were full of curiosity.

'Ingrid something – sounds Swedish.'

'What's she like?'

'No idea. We don't know a thing, except her name's up on the new House List downstairs. And she's marked down to be in Four Alpha, like the rest of us on this floor.'

'We could always find out,' said Jenny. 'We could go and ask Mrs Barry about her.'

But Rebecca and Tish were going for a swim. They ran all the way to the school beach huts with their swimming things. After the long, sticky car drive the blue water in Trebizon Bay was cool and delicious.

'Isn't this lovely?' said Tish, lying on her back in the sea and kicking, rising and falling on the small breakers near the shore. The sky above was all golden sunlit cloud. 'It's quite fun to be almost the first back.'

'Except I don't know if I'm going to last till tea-time,' said Rebecca, splashing on her front. The long car journey had taken away her appetite, but now it had come back and suddenly she felt very hungry. The school didn't provide lunch today because girls weren't really due back until shortly before tea-time. 'Shall we go to Cantoni's?'

'Mmmmm!' said Tish.

They came out of the sea soon after that and as they

walked back to the beach huts, Rebecca suddenly remembered Tish's mysterious talk about hockey and what Helen had said. Well, she was going to find out about that in a minute, just as soon as she could get some food and stop feeling hungry!

They queued up at Cantoni's, the summer beach café on the other side of the bay. It was still doing quite a good holiday trade. But they managed to get the last two sausage rolls, an apple pie and some chocolate. They ate the sausage rolls hungrily as soon as they'd paid for them and then raced each other across the golden sands towards the dunes at the back of the school grounds.

Rebecca flung herself down in a warm hollow. 'Let's break the pie with our hands and eat it here!' she shouted. Then, as Tish sat down beside her: 'Now, come *on*. What were you going to tell me? What's this about hockey and pieces of paper in the holidays, and a master plan? A master plan for what?'

Tish broke the apple pie in two carefully and smiled.

'For the seven-a-sides,' she said.

THREE

ENTER INGRID

Apparently there was going to be a national seven-a-side one-day hockey tournament in the Christmas holidays, for schoolgirl teams Under-15 – something never attempted before at this level of hockey. Twenty top schools would take part, all the matches to be played off in the one day. Miss Willis, the head of the games staff at Trebizon, had told Tish about it at an athletics meeting in the summer holidays.

'She's entered Trebizon and we've been accepted,' said Tish. 'Mainly because this year's Thirds and Fourths, who all qualify for Under-15 hockey, have such a lot of talent.'

'That's right! We won the West of England Junior Gold Cup when we were still in Juniper!' said Rebecca, basking in the reflected glory of that exciting season. It had been in her second term at Trebizon.

'And we didn't even have Joss. She had that bad back, remember.'

'Well, mind you, we still won't have Joss,' Rebecca pointed out.

'We will!' laughed Tish. 'She's flying home for the Christmas holidays and she can take part, she's allowed. Miss Willis has checked it all out!'

'Really?' exclaimed Rebecca.

'I've put her in at centre-forward,' grinned Tish. 'All part of the master plan, as Helen calls it.'

Now at last Rebecca realized what Helen had meant and what Tish had been up to. There was a unique system at Trebizon. The girls ran things, quite important things like this, at every stage up the school. If Tish were made the Fourth Year head of games she would be the person to pick the team for the Under-15 seven-a-sides in December. And, secretly, she already had it all worked out!

'But Tish, what did you mean when you said about me? I don't get it,' said Rebecca, thoughtfully. 'When we won the Gold Cup I wasn't even a reserve. You had eleven fantastic players in the team, not to mention two brilliant reserves. You thirteen are all still around, you haven't died or anything, *plus* Joss, you say. I make that fourteen, which is twice as many as you're going to need anyway.'

'We'll be taking ten to Gloucestershire,' said Tish, pedantically. 'Seven in the team and three subs. The list is in my trunk. It's all typed out, ready!'

The secret master plan!

'And just where do I come in?' asked Rebecca gently, as though humouring a child.

'Right inner,' said Tish.

'Oh, Tish, be *serious*!' laughed Rebecca.

'I'm perfectly serious,' said Tish. 'Want a bit of chocolate?'

Rebecca, who had been lying on her stomach with her cheek resting on a clump of marram grass, sat up then. She took the chocolate, put it in her mouth, then clasped her hands round her knees and gave Tish her full attention. What was all this about?

'The Gold Cup was conventional hockey. Eleven-a-side. We'll be playing those matches in term, yes. You probably won't be involved, I know. Not with all your tennis to think about. But the sevens is something different. We'll practise in our spare time, get it all together for the tournament. We'll get Miss Willis to coach us. Each of the subs can take it in turn to stand in for Joss, that'll keep them in trim.'

'But you can't put me in, Tish!' Rebecca protested. 'What about the people who are going in teams – in matches – all term? You'll have all those to pick from!'

Tish shook her head.

'Have you ever seen seven-a-side?' she asked Rebecca.

'Well, I remember seeing a game at Clare's junior school once. It was on a small pitch.' Rebecca frowned. 'It looked quite fun.'

'I mean the sort clubs play. On a full-size pitch,' said Tish. 'That's what this is going to be. Can you imagine what it's like? One person in goal and the other six having to cover an entire hockey pitch –'

'They must have to run themselves into the ground!' exclaimed Rebecca.

'They do!' laughed Tish. 'You're catching on, Rebeck. And can you imagine what the one day-er will be like? To get to the Final you've got to play about four solid hours of the hardest sort of hockey there is! It's not hockey, it's an endurance test!' Her black curly hair was all bouncy: she looked quite elated. 'Trust Queensbury to dream up something like this! Of course they're used to playing seven-a-side. They play mixed!'

'Queensbury?' said Rebecca suddenly. 'Is that where it's at?'

Queensbury Collegiate was a very large co-educational boarding school in Gloucestershire that specialized in sport. It was a huge modern place set in grounds of more than two hundred acres. Rebecca always passed it on the coach when she went to her grandmother's, most school holidays. Her grandmother, who lived in a small retirement bungalow in Gloucestershire, was Rebecca's official guardian in England when her parents were abroad.

'Oh, yes,' Tish was saying. 'Didn't I tell you? And of course I expect they want to show off. I expect they've dreamt the whole thing up just so they can win it. We'll show them!'

Rebecca's interest was quickening.

'That's just near my Gran's.'

It sounded marvellous fun. Tish and Joss – and Sue. Surely Sue would be part of Tish's master plan? She would definitely have been in Trebizon's Second Eleven by now, like Tish, if she didn't have to give so much time to her music. But she could find time for this! It would certainly liven up the holidays. And Gran could come and watch! She would love that – she was always so sad that she couldn't come and see any of the things that Rebecca was involved in at school, or meet her friends, because of the distance.

'You really think I ought to be in, then?' asked Rebecca, slowly. She knew that she was very, very fit because of all the tennis she played. She also knew that she was a very good sprinter. 'I'd have to brush up on my hockey skills!'

'Oh, yes, they come into it!' laughed Tish. 'Plenty of speed – but you've got to have the ball on the end of your stick!'

'I'd love to be able to tear around all over the pitch!' said Rebecca, suddenly. 'It's the hanging around waiting that I can't stand. I think I'm all right when there's some action –'

'There'll be plenty of that! Everyone runs everywhere, they have to. You'll be brilliant at it, Rebecca, I know you will.'

They stood up. It was time to get back to school.

'Well, count me in,' said Rebecca. She was beginning to feel really excited now. She'd quite forgotten that nothing was definite yet. 'Who else is going to be in the team? Can I see the list sometime?'

'Hey – I've got to be made head of games, first,' warned Tish. 'Strictly speaking there isn't a list, *yet*. This mustn't get around, whatever happens. The master plan as my dear sister calls it is dead controversial!'

'Of course you'll be head of games!' protested Rebecca. 'Miss Willis is taking that for granted, too, by the sound of it.'

'I'll show you and Sue the list, sometime. But nobody else.' Tish was quite firm. 'You know what happens if you count your chickens before they're hatched?'

Rebecca searched for an apt response.

'Your goose gets cooked?'

They both laughed. It seemed a good joke at the time. But it didn't seem so funny later.

'I wonder which juniors will be coming into Court?' Rebecca asked suddenly, as they re-entered the front door of the boarding house with their swimming things. 'Any idea? None of them seems to have arrived yet. I hope we get some nice ones.'

'I haven't a clue,' said Tish.

'Let's see. I suppose it's still the new system, the one they started last year.'

At one time girls had been allowed to choose their house. But because some always seemed more in demand than others, and this led to problems, a new system had been introduced with Rebecca's year. House places were now allocated in strict alphabetical order going straight down through the Alpha, Beta and Gamma streams of each Year Group. Some exceptions were made for sisters and family tradition and so forth, otherwise it was all quite strict.

It had been amazing that 'the six', as well as safely earning places in Three Alpha, all had surnames that fell into the first half of the alphabet. Just! So last year they'd all scraped into Court House together, although only after a big fright, as far as Rebecca was concerned.

'It'll be girls who were in Two Alpha last year, won't it,' Rebecca continued, trying to puzzle it out. She enjoyed hoarding scraps of information and working out problems in her head. 'The first twelve in alphabetical order.'

'The trouble is,' said Tish, 'I can never remember which of them were in Alpha and which in the other two streams. Oh, crikey, I hope we don't get Nicola Hodges.'

But Rebecca was reluctant to give up her interesting mental exercise.

'I'm pretty sure Rachel Milton was in Two Alpha and she's got Moyra in Court, so —'

'Look, I've got a better idea,' said Tish kindly. She had a very direct approach to problems and she was smiling her widest smile. 'The new House List will be stuck up on the notice-board, so if we really want to find out, why don't we just look at it?'

Rebecca ran ahead into the common room, laughing at herself, and looked.

'Rachel Milton *is* coming in!' she said triumphantly. 'Told you!'

She began to read the names out from the top, downwards – Brenda Burridge . . . Sheila Cummings . . . Wanda

Gorski ... they're going in Three Alpha then ... Lucy Hubbard ... oh yes, I should have thought of her ... no Nicola Hodges, hurray! ... Eleanor Keating ...'

Tish had just come in. She looked surprised.

'What?'

She hurried over and ran her eye quickly down the Third Year column.

'Oh!' Rebecca was looking at the next column. 'This must be the new girl who's coming on our floor. Look – Ingrid Larsson. Does sound Scandinavian, doesn't it? Maybe she'd like the single room, the one on its own. Probably would, being new.'

But Tish wasn't listening. She had turned away, looking thoughtful.

'What's wrong, Tish? Someone you don't like?'

Tish shrugged.

'No, of course not.' She raised a weak smile. 'Come on, let's get our stuff unpacked and put some posters up. The others'll be here soon!'

Rebecca wondered what it was about the House List that had given Tish such a surprise.

There was still no sign of the other four, but they had just got the posters up when Jenny put her head in at the door. She and Elizabeth were in a room at the front, overlooking the big gravelled forecourt.

'A Swedish car's just arrived! You should see it!'

Rebecca and Tish rushed out, along the corridor, and into Jenny and Elizabeth's room. Elizabeth had the sash window wide open and the four of them crowded round, leaning out over the sill to have a good look down below.

The foreign car had pulled up outside the front door of Court House, long and low and silvery with a pennant flying on its bonnet. A very distinguished-looking man with blond hair had opened the passenger door, gravely helping out a girl whose hair was even blonder than his own. She stepped out on to the gravel and drew herself up very erect as Mrs Barrington came hurrying from the direction of the private wing to greet them.

The girl was tall and slender and she was wearing a beautifully cut skirt and jacket in a shimmering ultra-marine blue. She wore her long hair coiled on top of her head, thus showing off her high cheekbones and finely chiselled features to perfection. There was a kind of dignity about her, an unsmiling dignity. Even viewed from this angle, the girls could see that she was beautiful.

'In an icy sort of way,' said Tish. 'The Ice Queen herself. She's even brought some skates.'

'Oh, Tish, what a strange description!' Rebecca laughed. 'You're just jealous!'

They watched as their housemistress led away the girl and her father, across to the private wing and around the corner. Presumably she was going to offer them tea, by way of a special welcome to the new girl.

Ingrid Larsson had entered their lives.

FOUR

EXIT MARA

'Oh, Tish, Rebecca, you are so *clever*!' shrieked Mara. She hugged them both. 'Look, Anestis – aren't they clever!'

Mara's brother couldn't get in the room because Sue, Margot and Elf were shoving their way in, heavily laden, in front of him. They'd come on the coach from Trebizon station, having reached Court House at exactly the same time as Mara, just arriving in her brother's car.

'I am *sure* they are very clever!' called the Greek boy. He was a student in England, at present on vacation, and right now anxious to be away. 'The new arrangements please everybody, yes?'

At that point he was almost knocked over by Ann Ferguson, Anne Finch and Aba Amori who were charging up and down the landing looking for a three-bedded room. The three As were determined not to be separated. In fact the whole of Court House was suddenly alive with the sound of pop music, running footsteps, babbling voices and people bagging rooms. The twelve new Thirds had arrived downstairs.

'I must go, Mara,' said Anestis.

She wormed her way out of the room, stepping over luggage to get at him and kissed him on both cheeks.

'No time for coffee?' Rebecca called from the doorway.

He turned round, swarthy and good-looking and blew her a kiss: 'Not even for you, my beautiful Rebecca!'

Rebecca giggled as she came back into the room.

'If he thinks I'm beautiful he should hang around till he sees Ingrid,' she told Sue.

'The Swedish car?' queried Sue, casually. She'd tossed her violin case on to the corner bed, the one next to Tish's, and was now bouncing lightly up and down on the mattress. 'Springs are a bit funny. Wonder who had it last year?'

'I shall have the bed in this corner, yes?' said Mara. 'Next to you, Rebecca.' She jumped up and down on it. 'Perfect!'

'Isn't this a brilliant arrangement!' exclaimed Elf, looking out through the doorway of the adjacent two-bedded room. There was a doorway but no door. 'All together. I'm letting Margot have the long thin bed –'

'And,' said the black girl, appearing at her shoulder, smiling, '*I'm* letting *her* have the short fat one.'

The six friends laughed and talked and sometimes squealed as they sorted out their luggage and argued over drawers and hanging space. They were supposed to be unpacked before the bell went for tea. At one stage Aba looked in to see them: 'You lot still together? So are we. We've got two rooms leading off each other, a double and a single – we all want the single!'

'So the three As are together and that's just one single left,' Rebecca calculated, when the Nigerian girl had gone. 'The one right on its own at the end of the corridor. I expect she'll like that.'

'Who?' asked Mara.

'The Swedish car,' interposed Sue. She was intrigued by the sound of the new girl.

'Hey! I've still got some chocolate!' said Tish, later.

They'd unpacked now and put their trunks in the corridor. They sat around on the beds in the larger room, all six of them, munching chocolate and just enjoying being together again.

Sue took her violin from its case and idly scraped the bow across the strings. Mara winced. 'Needs some rosin, Sue.' Sue got out the rosin and started to apply it, humming. Tish knelt on her bed and leant out of the window. 'It's going to be a balmy evening. Mmm. It's lovely at the back, overlooking the hens and Mrs Barry's washing. Peaceful.'

'More peaceful altogether up here,' Rebecca suddenly realized, now they'd all quietened down. She was lying on her back on her bed, hands behind her head, staring at a fly walking across the ceiling. 'It was all coming and going on the ground floor. Telephone, TV on in the common room, people always clattering up and down stairs.'

'Oh, sure,' said Margot, mimicking a nose-in-the-air face. 'The air's much more rarefied up here. We're Fourth Years now!'

'And we can disturb *them* now,' giggled Elf. 'Those insignificant little Thirds down *there*!'

It was a moment of contentment. The six felt very pleased with life as they waited for the bell to summon them to main school for tea. They listened to the clock on Sue's bedside locker ticking loudly.

And then they heard footsteps outside.

There was a knock. The door opened.

'Good afternoon, girls.'

They all scrambled up as the housemistress came into the room – 'Good afternoon, Mrs Barrington.'

Rebecca noticed that Mrs Barry was carrying an enormous expensive-looking tan and yellow suitcase. Strapped to the outside was a pair of long white leather ice-skating boots, with gleaming silver blades below. It was an odd, rather exotic, sight on a warm September afternoon.

The housemistress deposited the large case in the middle of the room.

'This is Ingrid's luggage.' She glanced behind her. 'Come in, please, Ingrid.'

The six stared first at the luggage, then at each other.

'I'd like you to meet Ingrid Larsson,' smiled Mrs Barrington. 'She's from Sweden –'

The girl in the blue suit walked in, very erect. A shaft of light played on her hair, making it shine, almost halo-like. She was even more beautiful, at close quarters. She was unsmiling, but not in an unfriendly way. Although the same age as the rest of them, she looked very cool and grown up. She reminded Rebecca of a famous model.

'How do you do,' said Ingrid, in careful, perfect English, spoken without an accent.

'Hi,' said Sue, the first to break the awkward silence. 'How do you like England?'

Ingrid graciously inclined her head in Sue's direction. 'I like it very much, thank you. It has been a very warm day, don't you think?'

'Now girls,' Mrs Barrington said, in a jolly tone of voice. 'One of you will have to move, I'm afraid. Ingrid is going into Four Alpha with you, although she's only with us for a term. Her father's attached to the Swedish Embassy here, just for four months. As the whole idea is to improve her English, we want her in with a crowd.'

Silence.

'One of you will have to move out. There's the single free,

at the end of the corridor.' She looked round at their blank faces and laughed. 'What's the matter? The new Fourth Years usually fight like cat and dog to get that one.' She glanced at Ingrid, before taking her leave. 'All right? I'll leave you to sort it out among yourselves. Oh, someone had better look after Ingrid properly for the first few days of term – Rebecca?'

'Er – yes, Mrs Barry,' said Rebecca. It had all been quite casual. 'Of course.'

Her first feeling was a natural one: relief. If she were supposed to be looking after Ingrid, then she could hardly be the one who had to get out of the room!

But then who?

As the door closed behind the housemistress, leaving Ingrid Larsson standing there in the middle of the room with her luggage, there was a strained silence.

Margot and Elf glanced at each other then sidled quietly off, through the opening and into their own room. If there had been a door, they would certainly have closed it.

'Sneaky!' muttered Tish, looking at Mara, sympathetically.

Mara just gazed at Tish, helplessly.

Sue started to hum, sat back down on the bed with the rotten springs and picked up her violin. She pushed her spectacles up her nose and then scraped her bow across the E string, which made a very high-pitched squeaky sound. 'Hmm, needs tuning,' she said. She busied herself adjusting the key of the E string, bringing her legs up on to the bed and tucking them beneath her, laying claim to her corner in clear terms.

Ingrid just stood there. It was embarrassing.

Tish flicked some imaginary dust off her bedside locker.

Rebecca carefully adjusted the little frame with the picture of Robbie, on hers.

Mara looked desolate.

Sue tried the E string again. It made a terrible noise, even worse than before.

'That is very interesting,' said the Swedish girl. 'You play the violin in the bedroom – ?'

Mara's face suddenly lit up, with hope. It was quite unmistakable.

'Perhaps –' she blurted out. 'Maybe it would be nice for Sue if –'

Sue looked at Mara, coolly.

'I like the violin very much,' said Ingrid Larsson, impassively. 'It is a very beautiful instrument.'

'Yes,' said Mara. Her shoulders slumped.

They could all hear the clock ticking again.

It was left to Tish to break the silence.

'Come on, Mara. You know what they say? Last in – first out.'

'Exactly!' exploded Sue.

'Of course,' said Mara, bowing to the inevitable. 'It is only fair, I'll get my trunk and move all my things. To – to the single room.'

The rest of the six helped Mara move.

It was a shame, but nothing could be done about it.

'Cheer up, Mara,' said Rebecca putting an arm round her shoulders. 'It's a lovely little room, and it won't change anything. Look, you lucky thing, you've got your own electric kettle! And anyway, it's only for a term.'

'A term!' wept Mara. 'A whole term.'

Ingrid Larsson couldn't have been more concerned.

'I feel very bad about this, Rebecca. To find that I am splitting up old friends –'

'Oh, it's not your fault, Ingrid,' said Sue.

'Of course not,' agreed Rebecca.

Tish merely muttered:

'What's wrong with your English, anyway? Sounds all right to me.'

But fortunately at that moment the tea bell sounded and, as far as Rebecca could tell, the remark was drowned.

FIVE

NEWS FOR REBECCA

Of course, Mara soon cheered up. At tea, over in the dining hall in main school, the other five made a great fuss of her.

The truth was that, with the exception of Tish, they were all feeling conscience-stricken now – all wondering if they were the one who should have offered to move, whatever the rights and wrongs of the situation. Even Sue. They'd hated seeing Mara so upset.

Rebecca, in fact, offered now.

'Oh, dear Rebecca, of course not!' said Mara. She was quite cheerful again and had asked for a second helping of scrambled eggs. 'I like my little room! Besides, Mrs Barry has told you to look after Ingrid. You are the last person who can move!'

'Well, that's what I thought at first,' said Rebecca, with a puzzled frown. 'But she doesn't seem to want to be looked after. In fact, she told me so.'

It was true. The new girl didn't seem to need anybody. She seemed remarkably cool and poised and self-sufficient. Rebecca had been most impressed by it. For a start she'd refused to let Rebecca escort her to the dining hall.

'Thank you, no. I have already taken tea.'

'But at least come and see where it is. And I'll introduce you to some of the other girls in Four Alpha. You don't have to eat anything if you're not hungry. We can eat yours!'

'You are very kind, but no. There are some things I would like to do. I must unpack my luggage and put all in good order.'

'Well, look, I'll meet you back here after tea, then,' Rebecca had suggested. 'I'll show you over the old building – it's really lovely, eighteenth century! And round the grounds and –'

'You are kind. You are trying to look after me. But that is not necessary. My evening is quite planned. I shall arrange my things and then I shall take a long bath and do my exercises. And after that I shall change into a plain outfit such as the trousers and go down the stairs and watch the television. It is down the stairs, yes? In the public room.'

'The common room.'

'The common room?' For the first time Ingrid had looked interested in what Rebecca was saying. 'You say the common room? Thank you, Rebecca. Thank you very much.'

Now, in the dining hall, Mara's warm brown eyes were fixed upon Rebecca.

'Even if Ingrid doesn't need looking after, you aren't going to move for *me*. None of you are, so that is that!'

'There's no point, anyway,' shrugged Tish, with her usual realism. 'It's you who should feel sorry for us, Mara, not the other way round. It's not going to be the same now we've got Ingrers in with us, so it doesn't make much odds who moves!'

At the end of the tea she said to Rebecca:

'What a shock, after all our rush to get the rooms, as well!'

'At least she doesn't seem to need *me*!' said Rebecca, wryly. 'Not exactly the clinging sort, is she?'

But all that was going to change.

After tea the six friends walked across the grounds to the school's sports centre. Some trees were already taking on their autumn tinges, dark gold, deep yellow, soft russet. Rebecca felt happy to be back. Tomorrow lessons would start and there would be all the hurly-burly of timetables and prep and activities, but this evening was their own.

The hockey nets were already up and some energetic Second Years were racing up and down East Pitch, practising passes. Inside the sports centre, on the big green baize board in the main foyer, Miss Willis had put up various typewritten notices.

'Yes, here it is – it's up,' said Sue eagerly. 'Lovely and blank, I'm glad to say!'

The notice said:

FOURTH YEAR HEAD OF GAMES

Nominations below, please, with at least five supporting signatures. We have a heavy programme of middle school hockey fixtures this term and have also entered Trebizon for a National Seven-a-Sides (Under-15) – a new event to be staged at Queensbury Collegiate in December.

Please, therefore, make your nomination by 6 p.m. Sunday, prior to formal appointment of your new Head in the gym at 6.30 p.m. In the event of more than one nomination, an election will take place at that time and voting will be by a show of hands.

Sara Willis

The six read the announcement right through.

'Seven-a-sides!' exclaimed Sue. 'That's interesting!'

Tish then told them all about it, but not about the 'master plan'. She sent Rebecca a warning glance and Rebecca remembered, with a feeling of excitement, that she and Sue were going to see the secret list, later!

'Sounds fun,' said Elf, though she and Margot and Mara weren't strong on hockey.

'Sounds terrific,' said Sue, thoughtfully. She missed playing in the Second Eleven, because of her music. 'David's done that.'

'Well, let's get Tish's name up so she can choose a good team then!' said Margot, taking a pen from her pocket. She wrote in large block capitals ISHBEL ANDERSON (Tish's proper name) and then they all signed in turn, underneath.

'Hey, don't take up so much room, or there won't be space for any other nominations,' said Tish.

'I rather hope there won't *be* any,' said an amused voice, behind them. 'You girls are really quite old enough to decide these things in a civilized way without a lot of razzmatazz and having to hold an election.'

Miss Willis had suddenly appeared from her small office. It opened off the main foyer of the sports centre. She looked crisp in a dark blue track suit, although her fair curly hair needed combing as usual.

'Please don't think I'm undemocratic, girls. You can have an election if you really must! May I grab you for a minute, Rebecca? Like to come into my office?'

'*We* don't want an election, Miss Willis!' Margot called out with a grin as the games teacher led Rebecca towards her office.

'Anything but!' said Elf, sanctimoniously.

'If anyone's daft enough to stand against Tish, that's their look out!' added Sue. She had once done so – and learnt her lesson! 'We'll be in the sports hall, Rebecca – okay!'

'See you!' said Rebecca. Her heart was thudding a little as she followed Sara Willis into the office. What was this going to be about – her tennis?

It was. And it was exciting news.

'The county have got all your competition results through and computed them. Those results have jumped you right into the A Squad – Under-14 girls. You're in at number five.'

'Number five!' gasped Rebecca. 'I knew I'd done well, but even so –'

'Get to number four and you'll have the chance to play for the county. You've been hoping for that for so long! You'll have to do it by Christmas, of course. After that, you go back down the ladder again.'

Rebecca nodded. Although her fourteenth birthday had been in the summer, she was classed as Under-14 until 31 December. After that she would be classed as an Under-16 and, against tougher opposition, would have to work for her county ranking all over again, in the new category.

'Oh, I must get to number four!' exclaimed Rebecca.

'I'm sure they'll want you to have a match,' smiled Miss Willis. 'Well done. But it's next year we have to look to. You'll have your usual county tennis training at Exonford this term –'

'Is it still Sunday fortnights?' Rebecca asked.

'Yes,' said Miss Willis. 'But it's not enough. I want to see you bridge the gap, now! You haven't much longer as an Under-14. Miss Darling is willing to give you private coaching. Would your parents be willing to pay for that?'

'I'll write to them!' exclaimed Rebecca. 'I'll write and ask them! This minute!'

'Off you go, then.' Sara Willis looked at Rebecca with friendly twinkly eyes. 'They'll be glad to hear your news. I wish I'd known yesterday and I could have phoned them in London. In the meantime, we'll take it they agree – and I'll ask Miss Darling to sort something out.'

'Oh, *thanks*, Miss Willis!'

Flushed with excitement Rebecca ran across to the big glass doors that led into the sports hall, intending to tell the others her news. But she saw that they were now in the middle of a game of badminton. She'd tell them later! First, she'd run back to the boarding house and write to her parents at once!

She hurried all the way back to Court House, then stopped inside the front door to get her breath back. Running in the boarding house was against the rules. She made her way steadily along the hall, towards the staircase. The common room door was open and she heard a high, tinkling laugh.

It was a lovely laugh, as delicate as sleigh bells, and she didn't recognize it.

She peered into the common room and saw Ingrid Larsson – she was actually laughing!

Ingrid was standing with her back to the window, talking to somebody out of Rebecca's line of vision. She wore beautifully tailored velvet slacks of a burgundy colour, with matching waistcoat and a white blouse with full sleeves and lacy ruffles at the throat. She looked very elegant. Her face was alight with laughter.

'What happened then?' she asked, with a fresh peal.

Rebecca was fascinated. She turned and started to walk up the stairs, wonderingly.

Then, reverberating from inside the common room she heard another laugh, much deeper.

She recognized it at once.

SIX

TISH WORRIED

'Robbie!' Rebecca called out in delight. 'Robbie?'

She turned and came running back down the stairs and he immediately appeared from the common room.

'Rebeck!'

'Robbie!'

She jumped down the last three stairs and he caught her in a great bear hug.

'I didn't expect to see you again before Saturday!' laughed Rebecca with pleasure. 'What are you *doing* here?'

'Waiting outside the dining hall, waiting over here! Where have you *been*? Ingrid here's been looking after me –' Ingrid had appeared in the hall. 'In fact I'd have given you up by now and gone back to Garth with my darn' tennis racket, except Ingrid told me to wait and made me a good cup of coffee!'

'I was sure you would come soon, Rebecca.'

Rebecca glanced at the Swedish girl, gratefully. She had hidden depths. But –

'*Tennis racket*, Robbie?' How was she supposed to know!

'Yes!'

'Let me fetch it!' said Ingrid, helpfully, disappearing into the common room and then returning with Robbie's racket. She gave it to him. 'Soon now it will be getting dark, yes?'

'It certainly will. Thanks, Ingrid. Want to play, Rebecca?'

What a question! She rushed upstairs and collected her tennis shoes, a box of balls and a racket, while Robbie waited below. She felt a surge of happiness. She would write to her parents, later, but in the meantime some tennis against Robbie was too good to miss. He was such a strong player, one of the few people around that Rebecca could really pit herself against, especially with Joss away in California. She knew too that rugby was the only thing he lived for at the moment, so she was very touched that he'd decided to give up his first evening back at Garth like this.

'Ingrid wants to come and watch you play, Rebecca,' said Robbie, as she returned downstairs.

'If you like!' Rebecca smiled at Ingrid, pleasurably taken aback. 'I hope you won't be bored.'

On the way to the staff tennis court, which Rebecca was allowed to use in the winter terms, she poured her news out to Robbie. Ingrid seemed determined not to intrude on them in any way and she made a point of walking a little way behind them, rather than alongside. It was sweet of her, Rebecca thought, although quite unnecessary.

'Clever Beck,' said Robbie, putting his arm round her shoulders, and holding her quite close as they walked along. 'I'm not in the least surprised. And I'm glad the school's decided to get behind you, this winter.' He put on a solemn face. 'I can get on and play rugby and stop feeling guilty.'

'Oh, Robbie!' Rebecca glanced up into his humorous brown eyes, affectionately. 'You've been terrific, and you know it!'

After they had played two strenuous sets of tennis the sun sank behind the school's clock tower, throwing the tennis court into deep shadow. They played on, however, until dusk made it impossible to see the ball.

'I'd better dash now!' Robbie exclaimed. 'I'll go and collect my bike –'

'Here is your bike, Robbie!' said a voice. 'It was getting late so I have been to the boarding house and brought it to you.'

Ingrid was wheeling Robbie's cycle along the path towards them. They had actually forgotten all about her and hadn't even noticed her slip away.

'Thanks, Ingrid!' exclaimed Robbie. 'That's really helpful!'

'You have lights?'

'Of course!' he laughed. Astride his bike, he switched them on. Then he twisted round to speak to Rebecca. 'You're coming on Saturday, aren't you? Match starts at 3 p.m.'

'I'll try and get on the GCSC bus – otherwise I'll cycle,' said Rebecca.

He started to pedal away.

'Robbie!' she called after him.

'Yes?' He halted, looking back.

'Shall I bring Biffy with me?'

'You'd better!' He laughed, but he looked pleased. 'You better *had* bring Biffy. I don't want to lose!'

'Who is Biffy, please?' asked Ingrid, as they walked back to Court House together.

'He's a sort of lucky mascot, just something Robbie knows about,' said Rebecca, slightly embarrassed. Biffy, in fact, was a well-worn teddy bear that Rebecca had found at home in the summer holidays. She'd been given him when she was three. She'd got into the habit of taking Biffy with her to tennis competitions this summer and getting Robbie to hold him while she played. The 'mascot' had brought her remarkably good luck. Both she and Robbie now regarded Biffy as a special friend.

They walked on in silence.

'What is the GCSC bus, please?' asked Ingrid, as they reached Court House.

'Oh that. It's just a nickname, really. The Garth College Supporters' Club bus.'

'Nickname? What is a nickname?'

Rebecca explained that and then went on to explain that Mr Douglas, their chemistry master, was a rugby enthusiast who liked to follow the fortunes of Garth's First XV. He took his minibus to their matches every Saturday afternoon and often on a Wednesday afternoon as well, which was the other match day. The bus was usually filled with girls who shared his enthusiasm.

'So it's nicknamed the GCSC bus,' Rebecca ended.

'Will you go many times to watch Robbie?' asked Ingrid as they stood in the hall. She looked up the stairs. 'It is late now, yes? Let us go up.'

Apparently, instead of preferring to be alone, Ingrid was now positively seeking her company. It was baffling! Rebecca didn't think it was particularly late and she could hear her friends laughing together in the common room, above the noise of the TV set. She was longing to tell them her news!

However, she went upstairs with Ingrid, instead.

Once inside the room, the Swedish girl picked up the photo of Robbie that stood on Rebecca's bedside locker. She relaxed her facial muscles sufficiently to give Rebecca a really beautiful smile. 'I saw his picture, so when he came here tonight I knew he was very special to you. That was why I was so worried when he did not want to wait for you.'

It was a rather brutal way of putting it. However –

'It was nice of you to make him coffee and everything,' Rebecca confessed.

'And will you go and watch him, every week?' asked Ingrid, returning to the subject of rugby.

Rebecca decided that she'd misjudged Ingrid. Beneath the cool, self-sufficient exterior she seemed to want to be friendly.

'I think he'd like me to, but I can't,' Rebecca confided in the Swedish girl. 'The trouble is there's going to be so much on this term. There's all my tennis for a start –'

'But that is very important, Rebecca! You are such a good player!' Ingrid said, her face lighting up. She looked quite radiant. 'I have been meaning to say this to you. You are lucky to have such talent. I do not play myself, but I would like to come and watch you play in matches.'

'Well, you can if you want,' said Rebecca, surprised and taken aback by such sudden effusiveness. To change the subject she asked Ingrid about her ice skates, which were now hanging on the end of her bed. 'You know there's an ice rink at Exonford? A coach goes there on Saturday afternoons.'

Ice skating was something Rebecca had never tried herself but a few of the girls at Trebizon went quite often.

'Yes. My father found that out!' said Ingrid. 'That is my sport, you see, Rebecca. Ice skating. I would like to go very much, but I would not like to go alone. Would you come with me?'

'Well, if I can,' said Rebecca, once again surprised. 'But –'

'Let us talk about Robbie again,' said Ingrid, curling up

on her bed, while Rebecca sat on the edge of hers, along-side. 'You say you have the tennis for a start. What other things –'

Rebecca was beginning to find Ingrid's interest in her quite difficult to resist.

'Well, maybe hockey, too –'

'You are good at hockey as well?' exclaimed Ingrid, admiringly. Neither of them heard the door open.

'You are going to be put in a team?'

'I think Tish is going to put me in something!' confided Rebecca. 'When she's made Head of Games –'

'For heaven's sake shut up, Rebecca!'

Rebecca spun round. Tish was standing in the doorway, looking worried. Sue was just behind her.

'Hallo, Ingrid!' said Sue, quickly smoothing things over. 'Hallo, Rebecca! Saw you playing tennis! What did Miss Willis want you for – ?'

But Ingrid appeared to notice nothing amiss. Now that the other two had arrived, she seemed to switch off. It was as though a curtain had suddenly dropped down in her mind. While Rebecca told the others all her tennis news and they clapped her on the back, Ingrid merely picked up a book, glanced at it idly, then put it down and yawned.

She then got off the bed. She took her nightclothes out from under the pillow, and then bent down to collect various exotic-looking containers from her locker. Bath oil. Face cream. Moisturizer. Skin toner. Talcum powder. All the most expensive varieties.

She glided out of the room, without even looking at Tish and Sue.

'I shall take a bath now.'

The door closed behind her.

'Hasn't she already had a bath?' asked Sue.

'Looks like she's having another,' said Tish, somewhat acidly. Then she turned to Rebecca. 'You weren't *telling* her, were you? About the seven-a-sides? You are a fool!'

'I shouldn't think she had any idea what Rebecca was talking about,' commented Sue. 'I certainly didn't! What's going on?'

Rebecca waited for Tish to explain, but she had gone silent.

'The list, Tish!' Rebecca reminded her. The three of them were alone together, at last. 'You know – the master plan! You can show us now – me and Sue. You promised you would. Come on, I'm sorry I put my foot in it, but she's gone now.'

Tish looked uneasy. Rebecca had the distinct impression that she had something on her mind. That she wasn't as pleased with her plan as she had been before and didn't want to show it to them any more.

But, of course, she had to!

'Master plan?' said Sue, her eyes big and round, behind her glasses. 'Tish, what is all this? I can't stand the suspense! Come on – show it to us, then – whatever it is!'

'Oh, all right then,' said Tish.

She still looked worried.

SEVEN

A FATAL FLAW

Tish took a thick sheet of blue paper out of her bedside locker. There was typewriting on it. She knew how to type and often used her sister's old typewriter at home.

It was the 'master plan'.

As Rebecca and Sue studied it carefully, they were at first surprised. It was, as Tish had said, controversial! It took the form of a public announcement although, of course, it was only pretend.

At home in the summer holidays, carried away with excitement, Tish had typed the whole thing out properly, as though she had already been made the Head of Games! It looked very official.

It was all rather exciting.

'I can see why you've put Rebecca in,' said Sue handsomely. 'That makes sense! And Eleanor, well she's just brilliant! With Joss back home to play centre forward, the forward line-up is going to be fantastic.'

'But why's Sue only a sub?' asked Rebecca. 'She's better than me.'

Rebecca looked at the sheet of paper again –

TREBIZON UNDER-15 TEAM FOR NATIONAL SEVEN-A-SIDES TOURNAMENT

I have now selected the team for the above tournament, as follows:-

GOALKEEPER:
Jenny Brook-Hayes

RIGHT BACK:
Aba Amori

LEFT BACK:
Laura Wilkins

CENTRE HALF:
Ishbel Anderson (Capt)

RIGHT INNER:
Rebecca Mason

CENTRE FORWARD:
Josselyn Vining

LEFT INNER:
Eleanor Keating

SUBSTITUTES: Susan Murdoch; Wanda Gorski; Sheila Cummings

There will be at least one practice a week, more after half-term.

All girls on the list please confirm that they will be free to

travel to Gloucestershire 17 December.

Ishbel Anderson
Ishbel Anderson

4th YEAR HEAD OF GAMES

'Not as fit though!' Sue said wryly. 'That's the reason, isn't it, Tish?'

Tish nodded.

'On the day we'll bring in subs all the time, you can in sevens – every time a goal's scored,' she said. 'You three subs are great players and you'll get plenty of action, but you won't have to run yourselves into the ground like the rest of us.'

'Won't have to come to all the practices, either,' agreed Sue. 'And, as far as I'm concerned that matters! We've got the House Music Cup this term *and* the Christmas Concert – oh, Tish, this is exciting! I do miss being in the teams sometimes!'

'But what about all the girls who *are* in the teams?' asked Rebecca, worriedly. Maybe the list was a bit too controversial! 'Apart from keeping Jenny in goal, you've dropped all our best defence players completely.'

'Joanna and Robert won't like it, Tish,' Sue warned. 'And I can't say I blame them.'

Joanna Thompson and Roberta Jones had played at right and left back in that famous team that had won the Junior Gold Cup and had stayed in school teams ever since. They were rock-solid defence players – it was difficult to get anything past those two.

'Laura's marvellous, of course,' mused Rebecca, 'and Aba's pretty good, too. But they both play wing half positions. They'd hate being backs anyway. And Jo and Robert will be furious!'

'Then they'll have to be furious!' said Tish, slightly on edge. 'They'd be hopeless, both of them. Much too slow for sevens. They'd drop dead with exhaustion. It's completely different playing back in sevens – much more running about – but Laura and Aba can do it, I know they can! I mean, look at the speed of them!'

The Nigerian girl and the girl in Tavistock House were two of the school's champion runners.

Rebecca and Sue soon realized that Tish had thought the whole thing out with great care and that her strategy was the right one. It had to be a very fast, fit, goal-scoring combination to survive such a gruelling tournament. A fast, attacking team that could stand the pace in what was a much more open game than conventional hockey. But with stamina as well.

'It's no use winning the opening rounds and then fading out later in the day!' said Tish. 'I mean, we want to go all the way through to the final and win, don't we!' She was quite elated again, for she could see that she'd convinced Rebecca and Sue. 'I think we *can* win, especially with Joss as well. I don't think even Queensbury can beat us!'

Then suddenly she subsided.

'So what's wrong, Tish?' asked Sue.

'You've convinced us!' said Rebecca. 'What more do you want?' Rebecca was by now very impressed with Tish's master plan.

'It's got a fatal flaw,' said Tish.

'Fatal flaw?' exclaimed Sue. 'What? You mean putting your two best friends in looks –'

'No, worse than that. Can't you *see* what's wrong?' asked Tish, giving a weak smile.

They pored over the list of names, wonderingly. But Rebecca was struck by that weak smile.

Tish had smiled like that quite recently! When? Suddenly she remembered. It was when she'd looked at the new House List, downstairs, and something had taken her by surprise.

'Oh, flip!' said Rebecca. 'Now I get it!'

'What?' shrieked Sue. 'I've looked at every single name and *I* can't see what's wrong –'

'*They're all in Court House!*' said Rebecca. 'That's it, isn't it, Tish? All except Laura Wilkins.'

Tish nodded. 'And Joss, of course,' she said.

'What, the three Third Years as well?' exclaimed Sue. 'Eleanor and Wanda and Sheila –'

'Yes,' said Tish, ruefully. 'I had no idea until I saw the new House List. But it looks bad, doesn't it?'

They thought about it for a while, hands cupping chins.

'Aren't there *any* changes you could make?' asked Sue,

nervously. 'I mean, what about Judy Sharp – she's in Norris –'

'Her ankle would never hold out,' said Tish glumly.

'Verity Williams, then!' suggested Rebecca. 'She's in Tavistock, with Laura. She's reliable –'

'Too cautious,' said Tish.

'Marjorie Spar?' asked Sue. 'She's in Chambers. Marjorie's good – lots of flair –'

'And lots of music practice, even more than you!' Tish pointed out. 'Doing two instruments now, isn't she? Honestly, d'you think I haven't racked my brains?'

They digested the situation. Tish really had got it all worked out.

'Well,' Rebecca said at last. 'If it's all Court House, it's all Court House. It's just an unfortunate coincidence. You can explain that –'

'Later on,' said Sue, cautiously. '*After* you've been made Head of Games.'

Tish immediately brightened up. 'Do you think they *will* accept it? Given time?'

'Given plenty of time,' said Rebecca. 'Yes.'

'Better not go showing that piece of paper around, Tish,' said Sue. 'Not yet.'

'Don't *worry*!' exclaimed Tish. 'I didn't even want to show *you* two once I realized –'

The door burst open and Ingrid walked back into the room, all glowing and peaceful after her bath. 'Quick, put it away!' hissed Sue.

Ingrid was looking at them. It made Tish nervous. She quickly folded up the blue sheet and stuffed it back in her locker. 'Stop staring!' she said.

'I was just looking at the clock,' said Ingrid, impassively. 'I am very tired now. Is it not time for all to go to bed?'

*

Over in Tavistock, in Room 8, they were drinking cocoa. Sarah Archer and Anne Brett, from Four Gamma, and Tara Snell, Verity Williams and Laura Wilkins, from Four Beta. The centre of attention was Laura Wilkins.

She was a long-legged red-haired girl, with a snub nose and freckles. As well as being pretty and exceptionally good at athletics and hockey, she also had a sweet temperament, and so was very popular all round.

'Oh, come on, Laura,' said Sarah Archer. 'Let's put you down!'

'Tish Anderson's lot have put her down already!' said Tara.

'And tried to scrawl all over the notice so there's no room for anyone else,' added Anne.

Laura just smiled and said: 'I think Tish would be better than me.'

'But don't you think Court ought to be taught a lesson?' asked Verity. 'They're so full of themselves. I think it was really mean the way they put Aba Amori up against you last term!'

'They try to win everything!'

'Well, I'd like to have been Head of Games in the summer term, I must admit,' said Laura. 'But Aba won and so that's just history. When it comes to hockey, I think it would be better for Tish to be in charge. I haven't got a clue about this seven-a-sides business, for a start —'

'Shouldn't think she has, either!' scoffed Tara. 'I expect she'll just put her friends in the team.'

'It's probably already fixed!' laughed Anne Brett. 'They have fantastic parties up at Queensbury.'

'Look, let's forget it,' Laura said, kindly but firmly. 'Tish was Head of Games that time we won the Junior Gold Cup,

55

and that's good enough for me. Apart from Joss Vining, she's the best.'

They drank their cocoa in silence after that, disappointment written all over their faces.

'You really won't be standing, then?' Verity said, at last.

'No, I suppose not,' said Laura. 'Not if Tish is standing.'

Ingrid went to bed first, and Margot and Elf went next. They'd been along the corridor with Mara, who'd been getting depressed all over again. But now they were tired, so they came through and said goodnight to Rebecca, then disappeared into their room.

Tish and Sue had gone off to get washed and changed into their night things. Rebecca, already in her dressing gown, was sitting by her locker scribbling a quick letter to her parents.

'There!' she said, licking the edge of the airmail form and sticking it down.

'When will the lights go out?' asked Ingrid anxiously. She was lying on her back in bed, gazing at the ceiling. She had been doing some deep breathing exercises. 'For the clear skin and the clear eyes it is necessary to have ten hours' sleep.'

'Won't be long now,' said Rebecca, smiling to herself. 'Tish and Sue'll be back in a minute.'

Ingrid turned her head on the pillow and glanced at the picture of Robbie on Rebecca's locker.

'Robbie Anderson is the brother of Titch, yes?' said Ingrid. She pronounced Tish that way.

'Yes.' Rebecca placed the air letter next to Robbie's photo. Then she hung up her dressing gown and climbed into bed.

'I hope the Andersons are a nice family,' said Ingrid

suddenly. 'I hope they are deserving of your friendship, Rebecca. Do you like them?'

'Of course I do,' yawned Rebecca. She was almost asleep. 'I mean Tish . . . Robbie . . . well . . .' A great feeling of warmth rushed through her. 'I love them both.'

Ingrid just stared at the ceiling and said nothing.

EIGHT

MINDER

The afternoons were hot, that first week back. One day a large bumblebee buzzed into their new form room, an elegant room on the first floor of old building, just as though it were midsummer.

Each girl had her own desk now that they were Fourth Years. Ingrid sat immediately in front of Rebecca, by the window, every so often gazing out at the blue sky and the big cedar tree by south courts. Like Rebecca she was taking German and French, as well as Latin. She displayed a natural brilliance at languages and got on very well with Herr Fischer and Monsieur Lafarge, a new French master. She didn't get on quite so well with Mr Pargiter, the Latin master, who seemed to prefer Rebecca.

'He talks all of the lesson about Roman times,' she complained.

'But that's what makes it interesting!' said Rebecca.

As soon as school ended Ingrid would disappear, off to soak up the sun somewhere. She would reappear in wrap-over beach robe and dark glasses, just before tea, gleaming with sun tan oil. She emerged from these sessions deeply tranquil. As she already had a perfect light golden tan, presumably acquired during the summer holidays, sun-worship was obviously a long-standing addiction.

Rebecca greatly welcomed these sun-bathing interludes of Ingrid's. They gave her some respite. Because, to Rebecca's continuing surprise, the Swedish girl had firmly attached herself to her 'minder', after all.

There were plenty of girls who would gladly have taken Ingrid under their wing. Her air of calm beauty was fascinating. From the moment she'd walked into assembly on the first morning of term, heads had turned and several girls had been really friendly towards her since.

However, with an impenetrable gaze, Ingrid Larsson ignored them all and sought only Rebecca's company, often with great persistence.

'I'm only going to phone Robbie, Ingrid, and then going over to the library to look something up.'

'Then you must let me come with you, Rebecca. Mrs Barrington said to you that you must look after me.'

'Oh, no, here comes Clinging Rose,' Tish would say (or 'Creeping Buttercup' or 'Climbing Ivy') much to Sue's disapproval and Mara's undisguised delight.

So it was a great relief to Rebecca that at least when Ingrid went sunbathing she insisted on going alone. She never dreamt that Ingrid was doing anything odd, or that Mrs Barrington would be furious about it.

'Mrs Barry wants to see you, Rebecca Mason,' said Margaret Exton, putting her head round the door of the room. It was early on the Friday evening and Ingrid was having one of her innumerable baths at the time. 'You're for it. She wants to see you in her sitting room.'

'What for?' exclaimed Rebecca. But the Fifth Year girl

just said: 'Better go and find out, hadn't you. Probably all that stupid noise you were making last night.'

'Why just you?' asked Sue, in dismay.

'Rebecca went to bed quite early!' said Margot, coming through from the next room.

'It's not fair,' said Elf.

Mara was with them. 'I shall kill Curly if Rebecca gets into trouble because of last night!' she exclaimed.

The six had had their Fourth Year friends over from Garth College the previous evening – Mike Brown, Chris Earl-Smith and Curly Watson, Mara's boy friend. They'd watched TV and then brought the boys upstairs to make them coffee – the Fourths had their own small Common room on the first floor. They'd talked and laughed a lot, so much so that Ingrid had come marching along there in her dressing gown, her face covered in some special cream that she put on at night, and said 'Sssh!'

Although it hadn't been at all late, Ingrid was strangely irritable. It made Rebecca feel guilty about neglecting her and in fact had quite spoiled things, so she had gone to bed shortly afterwards.

Later on Edwina Burton, the prefect on duty, had come and shoved the boys out, because Curly was playing a mouth organ, but there hadn't been any real trouble.

'Oh, it can't be anything to do with that!' said Tish.

It wasn't.

'Sit down, Rebecca,' said the housemistress, nodding to a small armchair with a loose chintz cover. Mrs Barrington was married to the school's Director of Music and they lived in the private wing, which connected up with the main boarding house.

Rebecca was alarmed to see that she was cross.

'I've had a long talk with Ingrid, the silly girl, and she's full of apologies. But really, Rebecca, I'm surprised that you've been leaving her to her own devices. You at least know the rules about going down to the town beach, and bikinis –'

'Ingrid's been wearing a bikini – on the town beach?' asked Rebecca wonderingly. 'I didn't know.'

'If you'd been taking any interest in her you *would* have known and could have stopped her,' said Mrs Barrington. 'And incidentally she's been conversing freely down there with any strange youth who happens to cross her path.'

Mrs Tarkus, a local busybody, had earlier telephoned Mrs Barrington with all this interesting information, sending the housemistress hotfoot down to the beach in question to yank Ingrid back to school. When Rebecca had seen Ingrid at tea-time, serene and sun-drenched as usual, she'd given away no hint of all this drama.

'I – I'm sorry, Mrs Barry,' mumbled Rebecca. 'I just had no idea –'

'Apparently she sunbathes in the nude in Sweden and was quite amazed when I told her we forbid bikinis here,' said Mrs Barrington, wryly. 'As for talking to strange youths, she simply couldn't understand my concern at all. She's so keen to get in conversation practice and in her innocence she saw nothing wrong with it. She said she expected English people to be reserved and it's been a very interesting experience meeting new people.'

Rebecca could almost hear Ingrid saying it, in that humourless way of hers. She smiled.

'Rebecca, I don't want Ingrid to have any more adventures like this,' said Mrs Barry sharply. 'She must find other amusements. I gather she's not interested in hockey or netball –'

'No, not in the least,' said Rebecca. She sighed. 'Or

swimming, or surfing, or badminton. She did say she'd like to watch me play tennis matches, sometime.'

'She must do things herself – find an outlet,' said Mrs Barry quickly. 'The first thing I want you to do is to take her ice-skating tomorrow. She says she would really love to go to the ice rink, as long as you take her . . .'

Rebecca's heart sank, remembering it was Robbie's match.

'But I can't skate! I haven't even got any ice skates!'

'You can hire some! And Ingrid can teach you. You'll enjoy it! It will be so nice if you accompany her.'

'But the crowd from Sterndale always go, Mrs Barry. And some from Tavistock. They go on the coach! She'll be perfectly all right!'

'She doesn't know any of them yet, Rebecca. What's the matter? You haven't got a tennis match, have you?'

'I was going to watch someone play rugby,' said Rebecca.

'There'll be another time,' said the housemistress, not unkindly. 'Look, Rebecca, I would like you to take Ingrid to the rink, at least for her first visit. She doesn't want to go unless she goes with you. She'll soon make some friends amongst the girls who skate here, but I think she needs a helping hand at this stage.'

Rebecca was silent and bit her lip.

'Now, come on, Rebecca. I can't force you, but I would like you to offer.'

'All right, then.'

She phoned Robbie straight away, from the pay phone under the stairs in Court House.

'I've said I'll take Ingrid ice-skating, Robbie.' She could tell he was hurt because he just said 'Oh.' And when she said: 'Mrs Barry thinks she needs some moral support,' he said in a disappointed voice: 'I needed moral support, too.'

But at the top of the stairs she met Ingrid, just coming back from her bath. When Rebecca mentioned their going to the ice rink together, Ingrid rewarded her with a smile of great beauty.

NINE

AT THE ICE RINK

At the ice rink next day, whatever kind of support Ingrid needed, Rebecca needed a lot more!

She kept skidding on her bottom until her clothes were quite damp with powdered ice.

At first, even standing up on these things that felt like a pair of carving knife blades seemed an impossible feat. They had the most alarming way of shooting from under her, as though they'd never been there in the first place, especially if she tried to stand up straight.

Ingrid was such an accomplished skater herself. It never occurred to her that Rebecca needed to be shown the absolute basics, such as making sure to lace her boots up very tightly and always leaning forward to keep her balance. She was hardly ready to leave the safety of the handrail at the side and skate out into the middle of a crowded ice rink!

'Come on, Rebecca, hold my hand – it is so easy – we shall skate along together –'

'Hee – lllppp!' yelled Rebecca.

'Oh dear. Now you have taken the fall again.'

After a few minutes of this, Rebecca begged Ingrid to go off and enjoy herself, explaining that she would prefer just to hang on to the side and quietly find out how to do it on her own.

The rail was a great comfort to Rebecca. She at once felt safer. In the company of a rather jolly woman, another complete beginner like herself, she began to feel less regretful about missing the rugby match. It would be fun to know how to skate!

On the way to Exonford Ingrid had told her, with quiet composure, how grateful she was not to be travelling alone, and how much she was looking forward to skating again. Although there were other Trebizon girls on the coach she had, as usual, ignored them and given Rebecca her undivided attention. 'I like you so much, Rebecca. You are always so kind to me.'

It was difficult not to warm a little to such grace, especially when Ingrid even remembered Robbie's match. It came to her quite suddenly when the coach passed a public park where some boys were playing soccer.

'Oh, Rebecca – was it today? It wasn't today, was it?'

'Yes. But it doesn't matter.'

'Oh, I have been so selfish! How self-centred you must think I am! What must you think of me?'

Then: 'What about Biffy the Bear? Will somebody take him?'

Ingrid looked so contrite that Rebecca immediately felt sorry for her and did her best to cheer her up.

She explained that Tish was going. A Second Eleven hockey practice had suddenly been cancelled and Tish had decided to go and see the rugby, mainly to watch Sue's brother Edward, who was also in the team. Tish rather liked Edward. Sue herself was going to be at orchestra. Rebecca had asked Tish to take Biffy along and wave him a few times at Robbie.

'Do you think she will remember?' Ingrid asked anxiously. 'I am not sure Titch will remember. You are romantic, Rebecca. But she thinks only about dull things. The hockey! Who is good – who is bad. Always hockey!'

It was true. Tish was rather obsessed with the subject just at present.

Before the end of the skating session, there were two developments that pleased Rebecca.

The first concerned herself. She suddenly got the hang of it. She found that she could let go of the barrier and, provided she kept close to it, ready to grab it if her balance went peculiar, she could actually move along on skates. She leant forward, weight first to the right and then to the left, right – left, right – left, she was moving! Faltering here and wobbling there, maybe, but skating nevertheless. It was very satisfying. She could skate!

Or so she thought.

The other development concerned Ingrid. At one point Rebecca had realized that a throng of ice-skaters had halted, gathered round the centre of the rink, watching the Swedish girl. She was spinning round and round in her beautiful patterned skating skirt, faster and faster until the coloured whorls of her skirt all fizzed together as if she were a humming top. It was a breathtaking sight. There was a spontaneous burst of applause when she had finished and Rebecca herself gasped with admiration.

But what really pleased her was to see Ingrid surrounded by Trebizon girls later on, over at the coffee bar – Tara Snell, Sarah Archer, Nicola Hodges, Helena King – a whole crowd of them had gathered around her. Ingrid was obviously basking in their admiration and was chattering away to them as though she'd known them all her life.

And when they got on the coach to go back to Trebizon, she whispered to Rebecca:

'Some of the girls would like me to sit with them, at the back. Should I, do you think?'

'Oh, yes, you must, if they've asked you!' said Rebecca, hardly able to conceal her pleasure. 'I'll just sit here and read, okay? I like it by the window.'

Ingrid retreated to the back and shortly afterwards the big coach juddered away from Exonford's central car park.

Rebecca took out her paperback and squirmed down comfortably in her seat, smiling to herself.

The situation was beginning to look hopeful.

It looked even better when they got back to Trebizon. Ingrid's new friends invited her back to one of the other boarding houses for tea. This was allowed at weekends, for Fourth Year and upwards.

Rebecca returned alone to Court House and met Tish, just coming back from the Garth College match, wheeling her bike.

'They lost,' she said wryly. 'I've been down town with Mike and Chris. They bought me coffee.'

They went upstairs to the room together and Rebecca glanced at the table. So Ingrid had been right!

'I'm not surprised they lost, Tish!' She picked up the little brown bear, with the torn ear and the missing arm, still lying where she'd put him out. 'You forgot Biffy.'

Tish just grinned. 'Sorry!' Then she shrugged.

'They lost 22 – 7. You can't tell me a one-armed bear could have done much about that!'

Rebecca laughed then – and told Tish the good news about Ingrid.

The six really enjoyed themselves at tea. It was the first meal they'd had together, without having to include Ingrid, since the beginning of term.

'You really think you're going to get her off your hands a bit now?' asked Elf.

'Think so,' said Rebecca.

It looked that way. After tea, they found Ingrid back in the room, hunting through her suitcase.

'There's a film over in the sports centre this evening,' Rebecca said dutifully. 'Want to come?'

'Thank you, but no.' Ingrid had taken a leather photo album out and was leafing through it eagerly. Rebecca caught a glimpse of pages of shots of Ingrid, skating. 'My new friends have asked to see all my ice-skating pictures. They have invited me to spend the evening with them.'

She went off looking happy.

Looking even happier, the six went over in a gang to the sports centre to watch the film. Afterwards, as they came out, Mara tiptoed across to the big notice-board in the foyer. She had looked there every day. There were still no new nominations up.

'You are safe, Tish!' she whispered, as they jostled their way out through the main doors. 'Nobody will stand against you now. Tomorrow you will be made Head of Games!'

The six friends chattered and laughed and danced along the lamplit path that wound its way across the darkened grounds. It would very soon be bedtime.

When they reached Court House, Rebecca hung back downstairs and then telephoned Robbie.

'I'm sorry you lost,' she said, when somebody had fetched him to the phone. 'I'm sorry Biffy couldn't come.'

'Can he come on Wednesday, instead?' asked Robbie. 'We're playing St Christopher's. We're really going to need him. It's away.'

'Oh, Robbie, I'm sure that he can!' said Rebecca. She felt a rush of relief. It looked as though she'd been forgiven! 'I know he's not doing anything on Wednesday! I'll get him booked on to the minibus. I'll go and see Mr Douglas tomorrow!'

'How did the skating go?'

'Fine! I think I've learnt to skate!'

When Rebecca went upstairs, Ingrid was already asleep.

All in all, the day had been a good one Rebecca decided, as she lay in bed later. Ingrid was going to be fine now. That had been a wise move of Mrs Barry's. Tomorrow Tish would be made Head of Games – then they could really get down to practising for the seven-a-sides! Gran would be pleased to hear about this . . . she must write to her . . . just as soon as things were definite . . . crikey, she was sleepy . . . thank goodness it was Sunday in the morning! She'd have a long lie-in.

But the lie-in never materialized. Early the next morning there was a loud crashing on the door.

TEN

WHISPER, WHISPER!

It sounded as though someone were trying to bash the door down. 'Wake up, you six!' yelled Aba.

The various huddled shapes in the various beds began to move. The door burst open and the tall Nigerian girl came in. She'd been for an early morning training run and was wearing a blue track suit with her county athletics colours on the sleeve. '*Listen, wake up. It's important!*'

'Hey!' complained Tish from under the blankets. 'It's Sunday.'

'What's happened?' exclaimed Rebecca, yawning and blinking.

Sue reached for her glasses. 'What's going on, Aba?'

Ingrid sat bolt upright in bed, looking like a startled mermaid. Her plaits had come out in the night and her long blonde hair cascaded everywhere. '*Is it fire?*'

'Tish!' Aba ran over to the bed and shook her shoulder.

'What?' Tish was wide awake. Margot and Elf came hurrying in from the room next door.

It was sensational news.

'Laura's standing against you! Her name's down!' Aba

was still out of breath. She'd run all the way from the sports centre. 'There's a whole crowd of them out putting up posters and stickers! They must have been up since dawn!'

'*You don't mean it!*' gasped Rebecca, scrambling out of bed.

'Who is Laura?' asked Ingrid in bewilderment, still sitting bolt upright in bed as Rebecca squeezed past her. 'What is happening? What does Laura do?'

'She plays hockey!' retorted Rebecca, over her shoulder.

'Hockey? Oh!' A look of boredom crossed Ingrid's face. She watched them, all gathering round Tish's bed in a great huddle. Hockey? What a fuss.

'Sssh, please!'

She snuggled back down under the blankets and tried to get off to sleep again.

The others washed and dressed. They all ran over to the sports centre to look for themselves and then returned to the big kitchen on the ground floor to cook some breakfast and hold a conference.

Aba had gone off to discuss things with the two Annes and make her own plans. She was very upset.

'Tavistock are just doing it for revenge,' she told them. 'Because I stood against Laura in the summer, and I won. Now they're trying to make things nasty for Tish. They're saying really nasty things. It's all my fault! They must have been planning and planning to get their own back.'

'Tish will beat Laura!' said Ann Ferguson scornfully.

'It's pathetic!' agreed Anne Finch. 'Let's make a poster of our own.'

Down in the kitchen, they were all talking at once. Only

Tish kept silent, frying up the sausages and eggs and looking thoughtful. Posters and lamp-post stickers had been scattered all along the route that led across the school grounds to the sports centre. They looked dashed-off and crude: DISH TISH; DOWN WITH COURT HOUSE; that sort of thing. It wasn't like Laura, somehow.

'What a sneaky way of going about things!' Sue was saying indignantly. 'Holding Laura's name back till the last minute –'

'They must have planned it all along!' interrupted Elf.

'– springing it on us at the last minute. They've had all week to work on an election campaign, when we didn't even know there was going to be an election!'

'And they've got a crowd of helpers! Third Years – from other houses!' exclaimed Rebecca. 'And it's not even their business. Third Years aren't allowed to vote tonight!'

It was seeing a crowd of new Third Years fly-posting the grounds early in the morning, while she was out jogging, that had given Aba the first shock. She'd raced over to the sports centre and there, sure enough, was Laura's nomination up on the board, with several signatures underneath. It must have gone up late last night!

'It's not fair!' said Margot.

'Tavistock are just dragging in anybody to help them get Laura in,' complained Elf. 'That's all wrong. Aba said she saw Nicola Hodges – she's in Norris and that's a fact!'

'Oh, her!' Tish spoke at last. 'But Rebeck's right. Third Years can't vote, so what does it matter? Only the Fourths. They'll make up their own minds.'

'But we can't take all this lying down!' Margot protested. 'We've got to retaliate! At least it's Sunday. There's time to make some posters –'

'You could get up a band, Sue!' said Elf enthusiastically. 'Let's have a cheerleader and march round the school grounds this afternoon!'

'*No!*' said Tish.

They both looked at her in surprise.

At that moment the kitchen door opened and some of Court's own new Third Years looked in. They were the three who'd been in Tish's team the year Trebizon won the Junior Gold cup – and they were bursting with indignation.

'Anyone who wants to stand against you's got a cheek, Tish!' said Wanda.

'Anyone except Joss Vining herself!' echoed Eleanor.

'Are you planning your campaign?' asked Sheila eagerly. 'We've come to offer help. We'll do *anything* –'

'Tear all their stickers down!'

'Stick up some of our own!'

'We're not planning a campaign,' said Tish abruptly. She looked uncomfortable. 'Look, there isn't going to be a campaign. Thanks, but that's definite.'

They started to protest. Sue and Rebecca exchanged glances.

'Don't argue!' said Rebecca. 'Tish knows what she's talking about. It's much better not to have a campaign this time. Just let people vote – just let the best person win.'

After they'd gone off grumbling Margot and Elf just gaped at the others in amazement.

'Are you crazy?' asked Margot. 'What's going on?'

'It – it's just awkward, that's all,' murmured Sue. She looked at Tish beseechingly. 'Isn't it Tish?'

'What's the big secret?' asked Elf, suspiciously. 'What do you three know that we don't know? Come on, Tish.

Out with it. And give us some food for goodness' sake!'

So of course, Tish just dished up the breakfast and explained about the master plan.

It took a long time for Tish to explain about the team she wanted for the seven-a-sides tournament, and why. Almost as long as it had taken to explain to Rebecca and Sue.

They were all so engrossed that none of them noticed the kitchen door open behind them, just a crack.

There was somebody outside, listening.

Margot and Elf, not having the same interest or expertise as Sue and Rebecca when it came to hockey matters, began to argue with Tish, even after she'd explained.

'Whatever you say, you can't pick the whole team from Court House!' said Margot.

'It looks terrible!' agreed Elf.

'I don't *care* what it looks like,' said Tish stubbornly. 'But that's why I can't have a campaign. I don't want Eleanor or Aba or Jenny – or you two,' she looked at Rebecca and Sue, 'getting implicated. Or anybody in Court House, come to that. Not the way my team's going to turn out!'

'We're implicated already,' Rebecca pointed out. 'We signed for your nomination. It's just – well, who'd have dreamt Laura would want to stand?'

'It does look bad,' said Sue. 'Now there's going to be an election!'

'Oh, cheer up, you two,' said Elf suddenly. She couldn't bear to see them looking so worried. 'Tish is right. No Court House campaign, nothing. Because that'd look even badder! If she wins, it's just got to be a natural selection!'

'Which she will,' said Margot, with feeling. '*Of course*

you'll win, Tish. And we'll keep your ideas secret. Won't we Elf?'

'Dead secret!' nodded Elf.

The door flew open and somebody burst in.

'Whisper, whisper!' she shouted angrily. 'Secret, secret!'

She was in her slippers and dressing gown, stamping one foot in tearful rage.

'I have been looking for you everywhere! All the excitements going on, I am the last person to hear! Nobody bothers to wake me up. I am just left out in the cold!'

The other five looked at each other in horror.

It was Mara. They'd clean forgotten about her!

Nothing like this had ever happened before. It had been simply the shock – the excitement – the rushing around!

'I've been standing outside this door for ten whole minutes!' choked Mara. 'Just waiting – just *waiting* – to see if any of you would remember that I even existed.'

They were still dumbstruck. In dismay, Tish glanced towards the empty frying pan. All the plates were empty now, too! They couldn't even share their sausages. Mara saw, and burst into tears.

'You didn't even cook me any breakfast!'

'Oh, *Mara*,' said Rebecca. 'Please don't . . . we feel awful . . .'

'It's the single room!' said Sue in despair. 'It's you being stuck away in that single room –'

It was just the worst thing to say. It enraged Mara further.

'You are all horrible!' She turned on Tish: 'If you are thinking I shall come to the election and vote for you, you are wrong! You have forgotten about me and I shall forget about you!'

She turned to leave, giving Tish a last smouldering look.

'With such secrets and things to hide,' she said darkly, 'perhaps it would be better if *nobody* voted for you.'

She walked out. They were left silent.

'Do you think she really meant it?' Rebecca asked Sue later.

'No, of course she didn't. Not Mara! Oh, it's so awful about the rooms, Rebecca. Isn't it?' Then, after a while, Sue added: 'Mara knows perfectly well that Tish is going to win the election by miles.'

'It feels really strange, not putting up stickers, or marching round with banners or anything, doesn't it?' said Rebecca. 'It's making the day drag a bit.'

'I've been sounding out a few people,' said Sue. 'I know Tish is going to win! She's playing it just right. In fact I can't think what possessed Laura to stand.'

'Nor me,' said Rebecca.

As it turned out, they did put up a poster. Just one. The two Annes had made a beautiful one and it seemed a pity to waste it. Laura's camp had been allowed to put one up inside the sports centre. It was a good likeness of Laura, painted by Verity Williams, who was an excellent artist. It carried the slogan: YOU CAN BE SURER OF LAURA.

The two Annes' poster just showed a girl scoring a goal and underneath the simple message: PLEASE VOTE FOR TISH ANDERSON.

So, after Tish had inspected and approved it, they all pinned it up alongside Laura's on the doors of the gym. The election would take place in there at 6.30 p.m. and every Fourth Year girl would pass through.

'It's just what's needed, isn't it?' said Rebecca, stepping back to admire it. 'A dignified announcement. A polite reminder to people to vote for Tish as they go into the gym.'

That was what it was when they left it, just after four o'clock.

It was something very different when they came back.

ELEVEN

A SENSATION
IS CAUSED

'Where's *Mara?*' Rebecca asked crossly, yet again. 'It's nearly half-past six. We'll *have* to go!'

They were still at Court House, all sitting on the stairs and waiting for Mara to come back. Tish was playing it very cool. She'd pretended she was in no hurry to get to the sports centre. 'I don't want to stand around over there looking eager. We'll just stroll over when it's time for the election.'

But secretly she'd been hoping that Mara would come back in time. She kept looking at the front door.

'It's no use, Tish. She's not coming,' said Sue. 'We'll have to go now.'

'She's still in a big sulk!' sighed Margot.

'Looks like it,' said Tish. She shrugged and got to her feet. 'Come on then. At least that's one vote I know I'm not getting.'

'Two!' said Rebecca sourly. 'Ingrid, remember?'

Earlier, when pressed, Ingrid had said with great seriousness: 'For me to vote would be very irresponsible, Rebecca. Besides, I'm going over to help Hilda Watkins with her

French prep.' Hilda was a Third Year who'd been at the ice rink. 'You must remember, Rebecca, I do not know one side of a hockey stick from the other. Side? Is that right? Or is it end?'

'End.'

'Thank you, Rebecca!'

Now, Tish just laughed. 'Oh, I don't care about Ingrid!'

The five friends left Court House, waved off by a crowd of the new Third Years. 'Good luck, Tish!' 'We know you're going to win!' 'Up with Court!'

The rest of the Fourth Years in Court House had gone on ahead.

Rebecca and Tish and Co. were just about the last to arrive at the sports centre. They entered the big foyer and passed the door of Miss Willis's office, which was open. She was on the phone, but she pressed the voice cut-out for a few moments and gave them a cheery wave. 'All ready for the election? I'll get along to the gym in about five minutes. They're making a lot of noise down there. Tell them to shut up.'

When they turned the corner, they saw that the double doors of the gym were half-open. There was a solid wedge of girls spilling right out of the gym and halfway up the corridor.

There was a great hubbub of excited chatter. Something was causing a sensation!

It was Tish's election poster.

'Here she comes!' yelled Roberta Jones.

It was suddenly unnerving.

As Tish advanced down the corridor, Rebecca on one side and Sue on the other, the three of them were loudly booed. The booing and jeering got louder and louder, reverberating in the big gym. Then, everybody turned their backs on them and pushed out of the corridor and into the gym so that the doors swung shut in their faces.

Rebecca froze as she saw a sheet of blue paper pinned to the middle of Tish's poster. Thick blue paper, with typewriting on it.

It was the thing that Tish had promised to hide! It should have been in her locker!

The mock announcement of the team for the national seven-a-sides – all typed out and signed by Tish! Rebecca blenched.

I have now selected the team for the above tournament, as follows . . .

Beyond the double doors, there could be heard great hoots of laughter, interspersed with more booing and catcalling. Tish had gone a sickly white.

Her four friends tightened round her in a protective knot.

'What made you put it up, Tish?' gasped Margot.

'You were going to keep it back –' exclaimed Elf.

Rebecca lunged forward and tore the blue sheet down.

'Tish didn't put it up! She wouldn't be so daft!'

'It's just a dirty trick!' exclaimed Sue. 'Somebody's been in our room! You *didn't* put it up, did you, Tish – ?'

Tish just looked stunned. She opened her mouth and closed it again.

'Of course she didn't!' said Rebecca, scornfully. 'Come on, you others. Let's try and explain.'

They all marched into the gym, Rebecca clasping the crumpled blue sheet. There was a sudden silence.

Joanna Thompson and some others came up to them.

'Is it a forgery, Rebecca?' asked the girl from Norris House anxiously.

'Of course it is!' cried Aba. 'Isn't it, Tish?'

'Tell them, Tish!' exclaimed Elizabeth Kendall. 'Tell them you didn't do it!'

A few yards away, Laura Wilkins stood in the middle of a crowd of supporters. She looked rather subdued, but her supporters looked triumphant.

'Of course she did it!' cried Anne Brett.

'She made a mistake – she put Laura in the team!' laughed Tara Snell.

'Laura can't be allowed to play in the national tournament – she's not in Court!' said Verity Williams, acidly.

The hubbub started again. Some girls from Sterndale started chanting and slow-handclapping:

Down with Court. Down with Court.

Ishbel Anderson's a rotten sport.

Judy Sharp, a great fan of Tish's in Norris House, shrieked above the din.

'*Come on, Tish! You tell them! Tell them you never typed out all that rubbish – !*'

There was a sudden hush.

Tish was still a sickly colour.

It was left to Rebecca to try and explain. She waved the blue sheet. She shouted:

'It isn't a real announcement! It's only a mock-up. It was meant to be private! It was something Tish typed out in the holidays, just thinking maybe –'

The rest of her words were drowned in a storm of booing and cat-calling.

So it wasn't a forgery! Tish Anderson had typed it out!

'Shame!'

'But it's a good team –' Rebecca cried out, helplessly.

'It would be the best team on the day, that's all!' yelled Sue, impatiently.

'That's right!' shouted Tara Snell. 'You two are in it!'

There were fresh gales of laughter. Tish just took Rebecca and Sue by the arm. 'Come on!' She shook her head, hopelessly. 'It's no good, is it?' Tish could see that even her strongest allies like Judy and Joanna and Aba and Elizabeth, were looking bewildered and upset.

Then the door opened and Miss Willis marched in, blowing two sharp blasts on her whistle.

'What a horrible racket!' she observed. She glared round the gym and waited for the girls to quieten down. 'You're supposed to be Fourth Years, not two year olds. What was all that about?' They fell silent.

'Right,' she said briskly. 'If you must have an election for Head of Games, then let's have it and get it over with.'

Voting was by a show of hands.

Miss Willis didn't like the result at all.

'Whatever's the matter? Why have some of you abstained? Why bother to come at all if you can't make your minds up? Now come on, I'm going to take the vote again.'

But it was still the same result.

Twenty-five votes for Laura Wilkins. Ten votes for Tish Anderson. Eighteen abstentions.

A tide of emotion against Tish Anderson had swept Laura Wilkins home to victory.

Miss Willis raised her eyebrows. Secretly she was very surprised. But she walked over to Laura, smiled and shook her hand. 'Congratulations, Laura. I now officially appoint you Fourth Year Head of Games. Come to my office when you're ready and we'll have a look at the programme.'

Laura looked pleased and proud, though a little over-whelmed.

Tish had now made a marvellous recovery and walked straight over to the victor.

'Lots of luck, Laura,' she said. 'Well done.'

'Thanks Tish.' Laura reddened. 'I – I expect I'll need it. But they all wanted me to stand.'

'It's just as well they did,' said Tish. 'They didn't like me or my plan one bit. If there'd been no election they'd have been stuck with me and they'd have been stuck with my plan. Because I promise you –' Tish allowed herself just one moment of anger: 'I'd never have changed it, Laura!'

'Phone for you, Rebecca!' called Eleanor Keating. They'd all walked back through the front door of Court House at that very moment. 'Did Tish win?' she asked eagerly, as she handed Rebecca the phone.

'Does it look like it?' asked Rebecca. A more doleful procession trudging into the downstairs common room to watch TV would have been hard to imagine.

'Hello?'

'Rebeck!'

Her spirits at once lifted. It was Robbie.

'Got on the bus for Wednesday, then?' he asked.

'The last seat!' said Rebecca. At least something had gone right today! She'd been over to Norris three times that morning, before catching Mr Douglas at home. His wife was the housemistress there and they had a flat at the back. He'd been out in his minibus, taking some of the Catholic girls to Mass in the town. To Rebecca's relief, there was a seat for the rugby matches going begging this term!

As Garth College were playing St Christopher's away, fifteen miles distant, it had to be the G C S C bus or nothing.

'I couldn't believe my luck!' Rebecca told Robbie. 'He's got all his regulars from last year and the bus would definitely be full, except Amanda Hancock's left! Did you know she got Fs and Gs in all her GCSEs again? Isn't that lucky!'

'Sounds like filthy luck to me,' laughed Robbie.

'Oh, *Robbie*!'

'So you've got her seat, then? Wednesdays and Saturdays for the rest of the term –?'

'Court House has!' nodded Rebecca. 'Mr Douglas said okay – Amanda was in Court, after all. When I can't use it maybe Tish can. Well, somebody can. I mean, Robbie, I haven't got my tennis schedule yet. But we'll make sure we hang on to the seat somehow, don't worry!'

'I bet Biffy's pleased!' said Robbie.

'Biffy is very pleased.'

'Hey, how did Tish get on today?' Robbie remembered. 'Somebody said there was an election after all.'

'She lost.' Rebecca told Robbie all about it, keeping her voice low.

'What, that list she was messing about with at home?' he asked in amazement. 'She put it up on display, before she'd even been voted in?' He whistled. 'Phew. Sometimes wonder if my sister's thick.'

'I'm sure *she* didn't,' said Rebecca.

'Well, who did? Got any ideas?'

'No!' Rebecca said sharply. It was too upsetting even to think about, let alone discuss.

Margot and Elf had no such qualms. They lay in wait for Mara and grabbed her as soon as she got back.

'Where've you been?'

'You realize Tish lost, don't you?'

'I don't believe you!' said Mara, looking suddenly panicky.

'Nobody voted for her, just as you wanted!' exclaimed Margot.

Mara looked so guilty, she *must* be the culprit!

'What's the matter with you, Mara?' asked Elf. 'What a crazy thing to do!'

'I – I –' Mara burst into tears.

Tish came out into the hall, with Rebecca and Sue just behind her.

'Leave Mara alone,' she said. 'What makes you think she did it? I might have put the team list up myself, for all you know.'

'But Tish. When we asked you that, you –' began Elf.

'I didn't reply, did I?' said Tish.

They all looked at her wonderingly.

'You mean you *did* put it up?' Sue exclaimed. 'You chucked everything away, just like that? You blew it?'

The very idea made Rebecca's senses reel.

But Tish was looking at Mara.

'You thought I should, didn't you Mara? It was the right thing to do, wasn't it?'

Margot and Elf were acutely embarrassed.

'Oh, Mara, sorry . . .'

'We didn't mean to accuse you.'

For the second time that day Mara flew into a rage. She lashed out in all directions.

'You *did* mean to accuse me! Of course you did! I don't know what you're talking about – I just know I don't like you any more, any of you! You have secrets from me now!'

She pushed past them and reached the foot of the staircase.

'Nothing is the same now you are all together, without me. It is like – it is like –'

Ingrid Larsson came gliding down the stairs, calm and lovely in a blue dress.

'Excuse me. Sssh, please. I am going to watch the TV.'

'– like the new Ice Age or something!' exclaimed Mara, running up the stairs to her room.

'Well, I like that!' exploded Rebecca. 'You did what she wanted, Tish, and she acts like that!'

'You fool, Tish!' said Sue. 'What on earth did you take any notice of Mara for? She doesn't know anything about hockey! Now you'll never ever be Head of Games because Joss will come back –'

'And we'll never win the seven-a-sides!' said Rebecca. 'Oh, Tish. It was going to be such fun trying.'

'Don't talk to me about Mara,' said Tish coldly.

The temperature was dropping fast.

TWELVE

TIME PASSES

'Tish, the whole idea was to keep it *secret*! Then you'd have won!' said Sue, at bedtime. 'Wouldn't she, Rebecca?'

They were perched on Rebecca's bed, eating peanuts. Tish had just had a shower and her damp curls lay flat to her head. In the next bed, Ingrid was trying to read a book and had her hands over her ears.

'But would that have been honest?' asked Tish. 'Mara didn't think so!'

'Oh, come *on*!' said Rebecca. 'Mara was just upset. She didn't really care!'

'She thought it was all wrong!' exploded Tish. 'That's obvious!'

'Obvious –?' protested Rebecca.

'Look, does it matter?' asked Tish. 'The point is maybe she was right. They tore me into tiny pieces, didn't they?' It had been a chastening experience.

'And us, too!' said Sue, with feeling. 'It's just great being made a laughing stock!'

'It was supposed to be a secret! You said you were going to keep it secret!' said Rebecca. She had never been so mystified. 'If you'd been made Head of Games, everything would have turned out all right. Can't you see that?'

'Yes, maybe it would.'

'It's no use looking sorry now!' said Sue.

Tish looked angry. She was about to say something.

But Ingrid suddenly took her hands from her ears and addressed them plaintively: 'Hockey. Always hockey!'

Tish then got up very slowly from the end of Rebecca's bed.

'I agree with you, Ingrid,' she said. 'As a topic of conversation it gets very boring.' She turned and looked at the other two, coldly. 'I really don't want to talk about it any more.'

After they were all in bed, Ingrid turned her head on the pillow and said:

'Was Titch serious about that, do you think, Rebecca?'

'Yes, I think she was.'

Ingrid gave a little sigh of relief. But Rebecca was still mystified.

After that, although it turned into an exciting term for Rebecca, things never quite settled down into the happy, easy-going pattern of previous terms. Tish felt cool towards Mara. She tried her best to hide it, but she couldn't. It made things awkward for all of them.

Mara, really such a warm person, began to draw apart from them. She was in the school choir and became very involved in a joint choral production with Garth College. At least this enabled her to see a lot of Curly, who was in the Garth choir. She began to get careless about her work, and keeping up with the Alpha stream. Her poor marks began to worry the others, but she tended to shrug off offers of help from Margot and Elf, preferring to spend more time on her own this term, playing her favourite tapes over and over again in the single room.

Tish was very busy. She threw herself into hockey with great energy. She'd now been made centre-half in the Trebizon Second Eleven, Laura Wilkins having come in at Tish's former wing-half position, and it was her secret ambition to get into the First Eleven before she was fifteen, something that only Joss Vining had ever achieved. Laura had a similar ambition.

Both girls were in the seven-a-sides squad, of course, and there were a lot of practices. These were going badly and secretly Tish raged at Laura's choice of team. 'It's hopeless!' she told Rebecca one weekend. 'It's just going to be a waste of time even going to Gloucestershire.'

Laura had offered Sue (but not Rebecca) a place in the squad. It was a sub's place and it was only on condition that she came to every practice. As this was quite impossible for Sue, she had to turn it down, bitterly disappointed. She threw herself into extra orchestra activities instead and spent most of her spare time at the Hilary Camberwell, the school's music block. This was because Ingrid wouldn't have Sue practising the violin in the room at any price, in spite of what she'd said at the beginning.

Rebecca herself played more tennis this term than she could ever have imagined.

So, all in all, the six seemed to drift apart for a while, which made Rebecca sad.

For Rebecca personally, there was one other shift in the pattern – quite a dramatic one. In a totally unexpected way she formed a bond with Ingrid Larsson. It was to do with Robbie and the fact that Ingrid became Rebecca's 'eyes and ears' as far as Robbie was concerned.

It was because of the tennis.

Mrs Devenshire, the school secretary, met Rebecca in the corridor on the morning after the election. She was smiling.

'Your father's telephoned, Rebecca. From Saudi Arabia! He agrees to you starting tennis coaching at once, and he'll pay the extra.'

'Oh! Then Mum and Dad got my letter!' said Rebecca, in delight.

'Miss Darling wants to speak to you about it in the lunch hour. She'll be at the sports centre.'

Greta Darling, a lady with short grey curly hair and a ramrod back, was a qualified tennis coach and also a Wimbledon umpire. She'd joined the games staff at Trebizon back in the summer term. Rebecca ran over to the sports centre immediately after lunch, feeling very excited.

'I've looked at my timetable, Rebecca, and I've looked at yours. It'll have to be Wednesday afternoons. We'll start this week.'

Rebecca's heart dropped to her boots. Robbie's rugby matches!

'Oh, that's my half-day –' she began.

'Well, it's mine as well!' said Miss Darling. 'But the intention is to take your tennis seriously. I'm going to find you some Saturday matches as well. I've been in touch with the Club in the town and they're finding you some adults to play against.' As Rebecca's face fell still further, she added: 'Don't be alarmed. It'll do your game a power of good. Exactly what you need at this stage. You'll be an Under-16 next year, remember. You've got to catch up!'

By lawn tennis standards, Rebecca had come into the game very late.

'Trust Miss Dreadful!' said Tish sympathetically, when Rebecca told her the news. 'Why couldn't she have arranged for you to miss some lessons instead!'

'Just when I'd bagged the seat on the GCSC bus!' exclaimed Rebecca. 'Just when I had it all organized.'

'Cheer up,' said Sue. 'You'd never have lasted in the supporters' club. You'd have got fed up, just hanging around freezing cold rugby pitches.'

Robbie was very disappointed.

'I'll come to some Saturday matches, Robbie. I promise,' said Rebecca. 'Whenever Miss Darling hasn't fixed up any games for me, I'll come and watch you!'

'Oh, that's what you say,' said Robbie. 'I expect somebody else will get your seat now.'

Rebecca was alarmed. She mustn't let that happen.

'We've got to keep it amongst ourselves!' Rebecca begged her friends. 'Couldn't one of you go on Wednesday, for a start?'

But they were all doing other things.

At least, thought Rebecca, she must try and keep that seat in Court House! Or else, sooner or later, a girl from another House would want to bag it – and Court would lose it altogether.

She asked all the new Third Years, but they weren't interested.

'I'm going to Gym Club,' said Lucy Hubbard.

Eleanor, Wanda and Sheila were all playing in a Third Eleven match.

'Anyway, the weather's turned horrible,' said Belinda Burridge, who didn't like games at all – playing them, or watching them. 'Who wants to get all muddy watching an old rugby match!'

'I'm sick in minibuses!' piped up someone else.

Up in the little common room at cocoa time, just when Rebecca was in despair, Ingrid came in. She'd been over at Norris House, listening to tapes with some of her new ice-skating friends. She actually came and sought Rebecca out.

'Margot said you wish to keep the seat in the bus warm. Is that correct expression, Rebecca? Would you like me to go to the match? I would find that interesting.'

'Would – would you really?' asked Rebecca in surprise.

'Of course. The game is not much played in Sweden.'

'You – you'll freeze to death!' exclaimed Elf, who had just been stuffing a chocolate biscuit into her mouth. Rebecca shot her a warning glance. 'But – I mean – terrifically interesting, Ingrid.'

'In Sweden we are used to the cold. It is not cold, just a little damp after all the sunshine last week.'

'It – it could easily be fine again by Wednesday,' said Rebecca encouragingly.

At bedtime Ingrid said: 'Also, I will take Biffy for you, Rebecca. I will not leave him behind, like Titch did.'

'Oh, Ingrid, thanks!'

In the morning, Ingrid asked Rebecca for Biffy and she produced the battered old brown bear from her locker. 'What is the colour of the rugby tops they wear?' she asked. 'The team that Robbie and Edward play in?' She had heard Tish talking about Edward sometimes.

'Red and yellow stripes!' Tish called out from across the room.

'May I borrow Biffy today?' Ingrid asked Rebecca mysteriously. 'I shall make a surprise.'

Late on Tuesday evening, she brought the bear back to the room. Mrs Dalzeil had found her some scraps of material and she had been very busy with a sewing machine, over in the home economics centre in main school.

'Oh, Ingrid! Doesn't he look cute!' cried Elf.

They all gathered round, admiringly.

Biffy was now sporting a red-and-yellow striped Garth

College rugby top, with a matching scarf wound round and round his neck.

'Terrific!' said Rebecca. She felt a renewed pang that she wouldn't be able to go and watch Robbie herself. 'You're a proper little Garth College mascot now, aren't you, Biffy!'

When they all went to bed, Sue whispered to Tish:

'Ingrid's getting a bit more human.'

Tish just grinned.

On Wednesday evening Rebecca met Ingrid off the minibus, at the back of Norris House.

'They won! Robbie scored a goal – no, a try, yes?' said Ingrid. She was still clutching Biffy.

Rebecca questioned her eagerly and Ingrid described in great detail how Robbie had run up the pitch, with three St Christopher boys trying to drag him down to the ground, had hung grimly on to the ball, finally breaking through and scoring. 'Oh, you should have been there, Rebecca!'

Robbie rang Rebecca later:

'It was Biffy coming that did it, Rebeck!' he said. 'But what about you? Coming Saturday? Can you make it? We're playing at home.'

'I'll be there, Robbie!'

But on Friday night Miss Darling told Rebecca that she'd arranged a singles for her with Mrs Doubleday on Saturday afternoon. Mrs Doubleday was a stout, formidable player who lived in the town and had won the area Women's Institute Tennis Cup for more years than anyone could remember. She would provide Rebecca with just the stern opposition she needed.

'She's absolutely delighted to be able to help, especially as you can play here on the staff court. I think we'll be able to count on her as a regular for you.'

Of course it meant that Rebecca once again couldn't go and watch the match.

'Did you enjoy it on Wednesday?' she asked Ingrid. 'You wouldn't like to go tomorrow as well, would you?'

'If you wish me to Rebecca. Certainly. I will take Biffy again for you.'

'Sure you wouldn't rather go to the ice rink, now you know a few people?'

'Another time, perhaps. It is very crowded. I much prefer to skate out of doors. If the ponds or the lakes freeze while I am at Trebizon – I shall teach you to skate out of doors, Rebecca. Without the crowds, you will enjoy it!'

'Not much chance of that before Christmas,' smiled Rebecca. 'And you have to go back to Sweden then.'

She felt grateful to Ingrid. She so much wanted to hang on to the seat in the bus, so that she could go and watch Robbie sometimes! She'd rather feared that one rugby match would be enough for Ingrid, and that she'd decide that the whole muddy mess was rather boring! And as nobody else in Court House wanted to take advantage of the seat, they'd easily lose it. Some of the girls in Sterndale this term were now clamouring to go, Rebecca had heard. Of course, Sterndale had a seat already but they'd love to be given another one!

However, as term went on, not only did Ingrid turn out dutifully for Rebecca time after time but she became a fervent rugby fan. Furthermore, after the matches she would describe to Rebecca, with patience and in some detail, every move that Robbie had made. It was a great comfort to Rebecca. It was the next best thing to being there herself, and it formed a special bond between her and Ingrid.

'They're getting quite thick, aren't they?' some people commented. But of course Rebecca's friends understood what it was all about.

For there was no longer any question of Rebecca herself having the chance to go to rugby matches. As far as Rebecca Mason, tennis player, was concerned, it was the most exciting term so far. The two hours coaching every Wednesday and the tough games with adults that Miss Darling arranged for her at weekends were starting to transform her game.

Just before half-term, after one of the Sunday county tennis training sessions in Exonford, Rebecca at last forced Ginny Powell to accept a challenge match.

The members of the county junior Under-14 'A' squad were subjected to a continuous process known as 'sifting', playing against each other to determine their ranking. Rebecca had come in at Number 5 but she had to get to Number 4 to play for the county. She'd been feeling for some time that she was now playing better than Ginny Powell, the current Number 4, and Ginny had been reluctant to give her the chance to prove it. But the pressure on Ginny to give Rebecca a match gradually mounted until she was forced to agree.

After a long, exciting struggle Rebecca won! The score was: 6-4, 6-7, 6-3.

She was then officially ranked at Number 4 in the county, Under-14 girls.

'Oh, Rebecca, I am so pleased for you!' said Ingrid, when she arrived back at school on the Sunday evening.

On the Monday morning, Miss Welbeck read it out in assembly and Rebecca's cheeks went hot with pride.

'Rebecca is now in the county team and will play for them after half-term. I'm sure she knows that we are all very proud of her and wish her great success now that she is making her very first appearance for the county.'

It was all very heady for Rebecca.

But after she'd spent half-term at her grandmother's and the coach passed Queensbury Collegiate on the way back she remembered the seven-a-sides.

Her grandmother, who had no car and didn't drive, had been rather sad when she'd kissed her goodbye: 'To think you'll be playing for the county and your Mum and Dad won't be in England to watch you. If only I could come and watch you myself, Rebecca! But I can't manage it, not at my age. It's too far. All these exciting things you're doing now, and no family to watch you!'

Rebecca remembered the forthcoming seven-a-sides tournament so close to her Gran's home, and she thought wistfully of what might have been.

As for Ingrid's surprising interest in rugby, some of the others were not very charitable about it.

They discussed it one Wednesday afternoon, very early in the term. It was over coffee in Fenners, at the top end of Trebizon High Street. Mara was with them, for once, with Curly – but Rebecca was having coaching with Miss Darling.

'Ingrid's gone off with the Supporters' Club again then!' laughed Sue.

'Did you see the shoes she was wearing when she got on the minibus?' said Mara. 'To wear such shoes on a dirty old rugby pitch!'

'But you must admit she's easier to live with since she discovered rugby!' said Elf. 'I haven't heard her say "Sssh!" for a week. She's more relaxed, somehow.'

'She goes Saturdays as well, instead of going to the

ice rink,' observed Margot. She laughed. 'I wonder why!'

'Not so many boys at the ice rink!' said Tish, halfway through a cream bun. 'I mean Ingrid's so peaceful and mysterious and we often wonder what she's thinking about. Well, I think she's thinking about boys.'

'Oh, yes,' nodded Mara. 'She likes boys very much.'

'You catty lot!' laughed Curly. 'What's wrong with that?'

'Nothing – but I'm serious!' grinned Tish. 'I'm not sure if Ingrid actually likes boys – I'm not sure she likes anyone – but I'm sure she's looking for a boyfriend. It matters to her. Now she's going to the Garth rugby all the time she's bound to find one. She's feeling more relaxed about life already. Just deciding which one to pick, maybe.'

'How long will it take?' asked Sue solemnly. 'Two weeks? Three weeks?'

'At the most!' nodded Mara.

They started to lay bets on it.

But they were wrong.

September, October, November came and went. The autumn leaves dropped, carpeting the school grounds, leaving a wintry landscape of bare, dark-brown trees.

The first week of December arrived and with it a big and sudden freeze, turning all the little streams and lakes around Trebizon to ice.

And in spite of all the bets Ingrid Larsson still hadn't bothered to acquire herself a boyfriend.

THIRTEEN

LAURA IS TROUBLED

It was very sudden, the arctic spell. November went out with storms and high winds but as they entered December, everything became very still and the temperature plummeted. The west country was gripped by the freak cold, twenty degrees of frost and clear starlit skies by night, then a strange, hazy-orange sun by day that had no warmth in it.

The countryside around became a lunar landscape. Fields that had flooded in the recent storms became solid sheets of ice, grassy hillsides lost their green lushness and became white and stiff with frost and along the narrow lanes the bushes rattled with tinkling icicles when cars brushed against them.

At Trebizon, everything seemed to freeze up. The pipes in Norris House, the water butt outside Court's back door, the little lake by the Hilary Camberwell Music School. The hockey pitches were rock hard and dangerous to play on. The frost lifted the surface of the staff tennis court and Rebecca was forbidden to use it.

Important hockey fixtures were cancelled and so were

Rebecca's last two matches as a member of the county Under-14 tennis team.

At both Trebizon and Garth College, the normal sports programme was brought to a standstill. In its place, a craze for ice-skating swept through both schools.

At Garth one of the rugby pitches had flooded and frozen over and the Sixth Formers begged and borrowed ice skates from all over the place and got up two ice hockey teams. They played every day, using ordinary hockey sticks. Robbie had sometimes skated on frozen gravel pits near the Andersons' home, wearing an ancient pair of Canadian speed skates passed on to him by his father. He asked Helen to send them down by rail and soon became one of the stars of the ice hockey sessions. Twice Rebecca went over to Garth with Ingrid and Laura to watch. Laura was friendly with a boy in Robbie's form called Justin. The ice hockey players soon became very fast and skilful.

'It's a pity we won't be wearing skates when we go to the sevens tournament,' Laura said hopelessly. 'If we go, that is.'

Rebecca knew that Laura had a crisis on her hands as far as the seven-a-sides team was concerned. She'd gathered so from Tish, who was rather tight-lipped about it all.

At Trebizon, it was figure skating that was all the rage. There were several good skaters in the school, but there was no doubt that it was Ingrid who had inspired this craze. She had brought no less than three skating outfits with her to Trebizon, each of them lovely, and every day she would perform dazzlingly on the small frozen lake in front of the Hilary Camberwell, watched by an admiring crowd.

Rebecca longed to try her hand at skating again, but ice skates were at a premium. She'd got hold of an old brown pair that fitted her – Mrs Barrington had found them in the attic – but they had to be repaired first. Rebecca had begged the shoemender to make the repair quickly, before a thaw came and all the ice disappeared.

But there was no sign of a thaw. The big freeze looked set in – and that was what brought Laura's problems to a head.

'It's hopeless having to practise indoors – this floor kills your feet!' scowled Roberta, on the Saturday, the fifth day of frozen hockey pitches. They were standing in the Sports hall. They'd just had an exhausting indoor practice match against one of the groups of senior girls who gave them regular games. 'This weather is just about *all* we need!'

'I don't notice you running about much, wherever we practise, Robert,' said Laura sharply.

'You must admit, Laura,' said Joanna Thompson crossly, 'it's been just one thing after another.'

Tish kept silent. She always did when these quarrels blew up.

It was quite true what Jo was saying.

Things had kept on going wrong for Laura.

When she'd first posted up her names for the seven-a-sides team, a great cheer had gone up.

There was Joss Vining, of course, and naturally Laura herself and Tish Anderson, both Second Eleven players. She'd then simply added the Third Eleven's outstanding defence combination – Jenny, Roberta and Joanna – in their customary positions. She'd completed the forward line with Marjorie Spar, the Third Eleven's best goal-scorer. As Sue had turned down the chance to be a substitute, Laura had decided to make do with just two. So she'd named the best all-round attack and the best all-round defence players from the Third Eleven: Judy Sharp and Verity Williams.

Her announcement looked like this:

```
UNDER-15 TEAM for SEVEN-A-SIDES TOURNAMENT

                    Goalkeeper
              JENNY BROOK-HAYES (Court)

    Right back                        Left back
ROBERTA JONES (Norris)        JOANNA THOMPSON (Norris)

                    Centre half
              ISHBEL ANDERSON (Court)

    Right inner                      Left inner
MARJORIE SPAR (Chambers)      LAURA WILKINS (Capt) (Tavistock)

                    Centre forward
              JOSSELYN VINING (Norris)

Substitutes   VERITY WILLIAMS (Tavistock); JUDITH SHARP (Norris)
```

'It's brilliant!' Tara Snell had proclaimed.

A lot of people had congratulated Laura for being so dynamic and decisive – she'd chosen her squad within an hour of being elected head of games and posted the announcement first thing on Monday morning.

'Good old Laura,' someone had said. 'Tish Anderson's favouritism left a nasty taste in the mouth – and now this has washed it clean away.'

It certainly looked good on paper – the best nine players there were, in the Under-15 age group, if you took them position by position. Anyway, certainly the best of the bunch who played regularly. Except for Joss, in the States at present, they were all in the school Elevens!

On top of that, all the Houses were represented, apart from Sterndale – and so was the Third Year. With Marjorie Spar on the list, they couldn't complain.

Finally, except for Verity, nobody there was a special friend of Laura's, or even in the same House.

'One thing you can say about Laura, she's completely fair,' Anne Brett had commented. 'Not like Tish Anderson!'

It looked good in theory, but it wasn't working out in practice – in *the* practices, in fact!

Roberta and Joanna weren't fast enough for sevens, out of their depth trying to play the open game demanded of them. Just as Tish had predicted. They tended to get exhausted and fed up. But Laura just closed her eyes to the problem. This was her team and she had to make it work!

It was also a mistake having only two substitutes. Judy Sharp took Joss Vining's place at centre forward for most of the term, but when November came she had to rest her ankle. She was a brilliant forward, with the one weakness that her right ankle tended to strain easily. This meant that Tish had to move to centre forward so that Verity could come in at centre half. Verity's stickwork was good but she couldn't move and turn fast enough to cover the ground.

Finally, as if things weren't bad enough, just before the big freeze up Marjorie Spar announced that she couldn't come to any more practices until after the Christmas concert. She was quite tearful about it, although it had been obvious to Sue for a long time that Marjorie was trying to do too much. Mr Barrington had finally put his foot down.

So now they were trying to struggle on with only six players, the icy weather had arrived, and morale was as low as it could possibly be. The Sixth Formers had run rings round them today. A bust-up was inevitable.

'If you ask me, Laura,' said Verity, 'I think the whole thing's a waste of time. It's a silly game, anyway. Proper hockey is much more fun. And anyway, I'd rather be out skating than tearing around inside this sweaty hall.'

'Why don't we just chuck it all in?' said Roberta. 'We've never played sevens before. Miss Willis never even asked us if we wanted to enter. We can just scratch!'

Jenny Brook-Hayes, the goalkeeper, usually so good-natured, suddenly snapped.

'It's all we can do, isn't it! Honestly, what a waste of time it's all been – all these practices, everything.' She turned towards Laura. The realization had been dawning on her for some time now. She didn't mean to blurt it out, but she couldn't help herself: 'If you ask me, Tish was right! We should have had a few athletes in the team! Rebecca – and Aba – and Eleanor Keating, she's a fantastic little runner!'

'Oh, we should, should we?' said Roberta.

'Yes, but it's a bit late now!' said Jenny.

Tish bit her lip.

Laura had suddenly gone pale and the other three all leapt to her defence, angrily.

'You *would* say that, you're in Court!' said Verity. 'You all think you're so marvellous. Tish's team wouldn't have been any better than Laura's!'

'Rebecca's opted for netball this term!' Joanna pointed out. 'And anyway the only thing she really cares about is tennis!'

'And Aba isn't even in the Third Eleven,' added Roberta.

Jenny was about to argue but Tish said sharply: 'Oh, let's drop it.'

'Yes, let's,' said Laura, turning on her heel. She looked troubled.

'Well, what d'you think we should do?' asked Verity, starting to follow her as she walked away. 'Do you think we should scratch?'

'Look, shut up about it,' said Laura. 'We're not going to

scratch. We can't! Not when we've got Joss coming back to play.'

Then she stopped dead and turned to face them. Tish was surprised to see her so angry.

'You've all got to start playing properly, that's what. We may not be able to win, but at least we're going to enter! You lot got me into this, so you can get me out!'

It was Verity she was looking at mainly.

While Tish had been over at the sports centre, Rebecca had rushed down to the town on her bike.

She had just come back and her wheels were crunching over the frosty gravel in front of Court House, when she caught sight of a track-suited Tish coming round the corner, deep in thought after what had taken place.

'Tish!' Rebecca cried joyfully. She was in her thick school cloak, with the hood up. The pair of brown skating boots was slung round her neck. 'I've got them! They're mended.'

She dismounted and scooted over to Tish.

'Robbie's phoned! The boys are going to have a skating party, on the common. The river's frozen all the way along! There'll be music and hot dogs and they're going to rig up some fairy lights for when it gets dark. Mrs Barry says we can go – What's the matter, Tish?'

'Nothing.'

'Oh, Tish – you *must* come!'

'You know I can't skate, Rebeck!'

'Well, neither can I!' laughed Rebecca. 'We can fall over together. Look, we've got to find some more skates from somewhere. You've *got* to come –'

'No, honestly, Rebeck. It doesn't matter.' Tish simply wasn't in the mood. But she managed to summon up a smile. 'Glad you got the skates back in time! Just make sure you bring me back a hot dog. And mind you don't fall over too many times!'

'Ingrid's asked if she can come!' said Rebecca. 'She says she wants to look after me, so I ought to be all right!'

FOURTEEN

THE ICE QUEEN

But how much longer was Ingrid going to take to get ready, wondered Rebecca. What was she *doing* up there? Mrs Barry would be getting the car out in a minute and then it would be time to go!

Rebecca herself had been ready for some time. She was getting uncomfortably hot sitting in the big common room downstairs, waiting for Ingrid. She'd put on her warmest clothes, all prepared for the skating party . . . thick sweaters, tweed skirt, woollen tights and fur boots, long knitted scarf wound round her neck. The brown skating boots were slung over her shoulder.

It seemed hours now since Ingrid had disappeared into the bathroom upstairs, with armfuls of clothes, her two hairbrushes, her combs . . . various little jars and an aerosol can of hair spray.

Suddenly Rebecca heard the car's engine outside. Mrs Barry was ready! She rushed out of the room and ran up the stairs in a slight panic, calling: 'Ingrid! *Ingrid!* Come on!'

When she got to the bathroom the door was swinging

open and all that was left in the empty room were the mingled scents of talcum powder, bath oil and hair spray.

'She's gone!' said Tish, when Rebecca looked into the room. Tish was kneeling on her bed, elbows on the sill, gazing through the window, which looked across to Norris House. She seemed to have been deep in thought. 'She went about ten minutes ago. Didn't you know? She got on the minibus with a crowd from Norris.'

'She's gone with Mr Douglas?' exclaimed Rebecca in surprise. 'Oh, I've been waiting for her!'

She hurried downstairs and got into Mrs Barrington's car.

'We'll have to drive slowly, Rebecca. The roads are icing up again as fast as they grit them.'

When the housemistress dropped her on the common, the scene took Rebecca's breath away.

Figures were skating on the frozen river, against a pink winter sky and a great hazy-orange sun. It was sinking fast. Some of the boys had set up a barbecue on the bank and there was the faint smell of wood smoke and sausages frying. Justin Thomas was skating slowly along at the edge of the ice, playing an accordion, a rather melancholy, haunting little tune. Somebody had just turned on the fairy lights which were strung out between a row of bent little willow trees along the river.

It was a romantic sight and stirred Rebecca deeply.

She drew nearer, crunching over the frosty grass, scanning all the skaters and looking for Robbie. It was high up on the common. The air itself was like cold ice as she inhaled it. When she exhaled her own warm breath condensed like a great cloud of cigarette smoke in front of her.

She couldn't see Robbie, but she wasn't too surprised. She'd arrived late and he loved those old speed skates. The winding course of the frozen river, wending its way mistily through the trees into the distance, would be irresistible to him. He would probably be hurtling along it right now, as fast as he could go, coming back to look for her from time to time.

She sat on a log underneath the fairy lights and started to put her skating boots on. She had just finished tightening the laces when suddenly she saw Ingrid.

It was the laugh she heard first, high and tinkling, gently teasing somebody. Then Rebecca heard the rustle of branches, just a little way along the river bank from where she sat, and saw a figure come skating out from beneath a cluster of overhanging bushes, leaning backwards into a figure of eight. Her hands were locked together in a big white fur muff.

Rebecca caught just a glimpse of the mysterious smile and the flash of cold blue eyes beneath the crown of coiled hair, which tonight seemed to throw off the silvery glitter of the ice itself.

Then she turned and headed away up river. Her school cloak was somehow transformed; now a queenly robe, rippling behind her as she floated off into the distance.

Rebecca suddenly remembered what Tish had called Ingrid.

The Ice Queen!

A sudden little chill ran through her as she heard a voice in the bushes shout –

'Coming!'

There was a crashing of branches and then Robbie shot out on to the ice, braked his speed skates, turned, then headed off up river in pursuit of Ingrid.

Rebecca stood up carefully on her skates and then walked gingerly on to the ice. 'Robbie!' she called out anxiously. '*Robbie!* It's me – Rebecca.'

Heads turned and people were looking at her. But Robbie didn't seem to hear. He was almost bent double now, head low like a charging bull, accelerating in pursuit of Ingrid who had already disappeared round the first bend in the river.

'Robbie!'

Rebecca started to move forward on the skates, flailing her arms to keep her balance. She must remember not to lean backwards, or she would fall. Push her weight forward, first with the right foot, then with the left. *'Robbie! Come back!'* People were still looking at her but she didn't care.

She must catch up with Robbie!

He had vanished round the bend.

She was going fast now, faster and faster, veering crazily to the right and then crazily to the left. She was frightened. It was so different from the ice rink, enclosed and safe. There was nothing to grab hold of – no handrail! – nothing to make her feel secure. She was going fast and she didn't know how to stop!

She streaked round the bend and saw that they'd both disappeared. She was hurtling along the straight when she saw, too late, the trailing branches ahead, half buried in ice. She tried to avoid them – and crashed into a steep wall of river bank. The force of the impact knocked all the breath from her body. She sprawled, winded, her face against a frosty tussock.

Then from over the top of the bank she heard the faint sound of laughter again.

She pulled herself up the bank and looked through a screen of frozen fronds. They'd skated round into a back-water that doubled back behind the river, a frozen little wasteland of ice that ran amongst bare trees. She could see them beyond the trees.

Ingrid had let her cloak drop down on to the ice. She was wearing a new red skating dress, trimmed with white, and still had one hand in her muff. She was laughing and letting Robbie lift her high in the air.

He started to laugh, too – gazing up into her face. At that moment nobody but Ingrid existed for Robbie.

'Now I've caught you I shall kiss you!'

Rebecca closed her eyes and pressed her hands over her ears. Then she worked her way backwards down the steep bank until the serrated steel at the tips of her ice blades touched down on the glassy face of the river.

As they did so, all the feeling she'd ever had for Robbie seemed to run right out of her, down through her toes and into the ice below.

It also dawned upon her that Ingrid had been rather hoping to steal Robbie, all along.

Laura and Justin had come to look for Rebecca. They found her walking back round the bend in the river in her stock-inged feet, her skating boots hung round her neck. Her ribs felt bruised and she'd completely lost her nerve for ice-skating. Laura knew what had happened and she could see that Rebecca had been crying.

'Come and have a hot dog, Rebecca.'

'I want to go back,' said Rebecca.

So did Laura. She wasn't enjoying herself at all this evening. She looked at Justin.

'Drive us back, Just.'

He was seventeen and had just got his driving licence and borrowed a car for the evening.

The two girls sat in the back while he drove, because Laura wanted to talk to Rebecca.

'She's horrible, isn't she?' she whispered. 'Ingrid.'

Rebecca said nothing. She was far away.

'I feel ashamed now,' said Laura. 'About Tish. She should have been head of games, not me.'

'What's that got to do with Ingrid?' asked Rebecca, coming to. 'They all wanted you to stand.'

'She put them up to it!' said Laura. 'I didn't find out till afterwards. It was she who told them about Tish and her Court House team. Verity came and told *me* the night before the election. She wouldn't tell me how she knew, but she begged me to stand.'

So that was why the election campaign was sprung at the last minute!

'I was crazy to stand,' said Laura. 'But it seemed so wrong of Tish. Not a bit like her. Now I realize her team would have been okay. Much better than mine.' She looked utterly dejected. 'I'd change it tomorrow, if I thought it would be any use. But it's too late now.'

'Yes, much,' said Rebecca. Eleanor might be all right, but she and Sue and Aba had hardly played hockey at all this term. They were very rusty. The tournament was only thirteen days off – and anyway the hockey pitches were all frozen up.

'So that's that,' sighed Laura.

'I wonder why Ingrid did it?' Rebecca mused.

'I'll tell you in a minute. But, by the way, she put Tish's list up as well – she got it out of her locker,' said Laura. 'That's something else I found out.'

'Are you sure?' It took Rebecca a few minutes to digest this amazing piece of news. 'Tish pretended to us she'd put it up herself.'

'Did she?' said Laura. 'Just keeping her end up, I suppose.'

'No!' Rebecca said suddenly. 'I think I know the reason! Oh, that's terrible . . .'

Poor Mara! So that was why Tish had been so cool towards her, all term. Tish was convinced that Mara had put the list up!

Rebecca thought to herself: *Tish knew we'd hate Mara if we knew, so she decided to cover up for her. But in her heart, however hard she tried, she's never been able to forgive Mara for doing that!*

But Mara hadn't done it!

'Ingrid's got a lot to answer for,' said Rebecca furiously, thinking of the coolness and dissension amongst them in Court House this term.

After a while she returned to her original question. 'But why? Why should she even have *cared*!'

'She didn't,' said Laura. 'According to Verity, it was just that it got on her nerves. The hockey talk in the room. She said it would drive her crazy if you were all going to be in some tournament together. She didn't care about the principle or anything. It was all quite casual, quite cruel.'

'Yes,' said Rebecca. 'I can see that. That would be Ingrid's style.'

The Ice Queen, she thought. *Turning everything to ice.*

FIFTEEN

TOGETHER AGAIN

After she'd left Rebecca at the skating party, Mrs Barrington had returned to main school. She'd been asked to go to a staff meeting about end-of-term reports. Miss Magg, Four Alpha's form teacher this year, was apparently concerned about a girl in Court House.

'Mara's work has really gone downhill, Joan,' she said. 'We may seriously have to think about moving her to Four Beta. She hasn't any problems, has she?'

'I think having to split up from her friends and make way for the Swedish girl unsettled her back in September,' said Court's housemistress. 'But she'll have got over that by now! A lot of the girls fight to get a single room! Ingrid's father wanted her to share, of course. She's only here for the term.'

'Well, I'll mark Mara down tentatively for Four Beta. It's worked very well for Jane Bowen,' said Miss Gates, the senior mistress. 'We'll give it till the end of term in case she suddenly pulls her socks up – but that's only twelve days away!'

'She's been very involved with the choir this term,' Mrs

Barrington said quickly, suddenly feeling protective. 'She's always worked well before.'

'Yes, but the work gets harder when they go into the Fourth and start working for G C S E. It tends to sort out the sheep from the goats,' said Miss Gates, drily. 'We'll have to see.'

The staff meeting went on for a long time, but even so Mrs Barrington was surprised when she returned to Court House to see that Rebecca Mason was back so early. She was talking to somebody on the phone under the stairs. She looked rather pale, Mrs Barry thought, and was holding that old teddy bear of hers.

Rebecca had taken Biffy out of her locker when she'd got back and had been sitting on her bed looking at him. There'd been nobody upstairs, but after a while Lucy Hubbard had come to fetch her down to the telephone.

To Rebecca's surprise, it was Robbie on the phone.

The boys who cooked the hot dogs had told him that Rebecca had been to the party and gone away again. He'd thrust a hot dog into Ingrid's hand, made an excuse and left. He'd cycled straight back to Syon House and phoned.

'Ingrid said she wasn't sure if you were coming or not,' said Robbie accusingly.

'And you really believed her!' said Rebecca, dully.

'Of course I believed her!' snapped Robbie. 'After all, you've been doing it all term.'

'Doing what all term?'

'Sending Ingrid in your place. I thought it was about time I made the best of it.'

'So I gathered,' said Rebecca. There was a physical pain in the middle of her chest somewhere. 'You're welcome, Robbie.' She put the phone down, click.

She walked down the hall, to return upstairs, then realized that she was still holding Biffy. He was in his Garth College colours, as made by Ingrid.

Rebecca went outside. It was a clear starlit night again, very cold. She ran across the frosty gravel, took hold of Biffy by his good arm, and hurled him towards the bushes. Then she ran back indoors.

She went upstairs and made herself a cup of coffee and waited for her friends to come in. She was waiting especially for Tish and Mara.

Rebecca had guessed right.

Tish had thought all term that it was Mara who'd taken the 'master plan' out of her locker and put it on public display. At first she'd tried hard to understand. She didn't want the others to hate Mara for it and had covered up for her. But the more things had gone wrong with Laura's team, the more Tish had smouldered inside and felt angry with Mara for interfering and losing her the election. Apart from anything else it had seemed such a strange way for Mara to behave that she'd wondered if she could ever trust her again.

'You thought *I* was behaving strangely!' exclaimed Mara, with great emotion and tearfulness. Then she started to laugh, with amazement and relief. 'I thought *you* had gone completely crazy, Tish! That you should hate me so much, because of one bad mood. Just because I didn't come and vote for you that day! As if my one little vote could have made any difference. I could not understand why you were being so stupid. Now I understand everything.'

There was a great suffusion of joy in the room; a return of warmth. The other three hugged Mara and made a fuss of her. Then, through the window, Tish saw the lights of the minibus over at Norris.

'Ingrid's just got back! She'll be here in a minute. I'm not sleeping in the same room as her –'

At that moment Margot and Elf came into the room. They'd been to the Saturday film and on the way back had overheard Nicola Hodges spreading the news about Robbie and Ingrid. Nicola had been at the ice-skating party.

'I should think Rebecca feels that way too,' said Margot, meaningfully. 'After what happened tonight.'

'Poor Rebecca!' said Elf, with feeling. 'Robbie must be mad if he prefers Ingrid to you.'

As Tish, Sue and Mara stared at Rebecca in disbelief, she quickly turned away.

'I think I'll go and have a bath,' she said. She went and got her night things. 'I must admit I don't particularly want to see Ingrid.'

When Ingrid walked into the room, five minutes later, Tish said witheringly:

'None of us wants you in this room any more. We don't like people who go poking around and taking things from our lockers and showing them to everybody.'

Ingrid frowned for a moment and then remembered. 'Huh! Not the hockey again!'

She turned on Tish. She was in a very bad temper herself.

'As it so happens, Titch, I have myself just seen Mrs Barrington and requested that I leave this room at once. Tonight. She says I may do so if Mara is willing to exchange.'

Mara's brown eyes immediately shone bright.

'Good riddance,' said Tish. 'I'm certainly going to tell my brother what you're like.'

'You can tell your brother what you wish,' said Ingrid. She was already starting to bundle her things together. 'If you think I would want to stay in the same room as the sister of Robbie Anderson, you are much mistaken.'

She stared at Tish icily.

'Your brother left me to pay for my own food tonight. He is a rude and ill-mannered pig.'

'Oh, I could have told you that,' said Tish.

When Rebecca finally emerged from the bathroom, there was luggage strewn all over the landing and much laughter and celebratory noise. Ingrid had already moved out and Mara was now moving in. The six were together again!

Hearing the joyous din, from the bottom of the stairs, Joan Barrington frowned thoughtfully. She made a mental note to see Miss Gates on Monday and tell her not to be too hard on Mara. It looked as though there might have been special problems in Court House this term, after all.

At cocoa time she went up to the little common room and said to them: 'I hope Ingrid's last ten days at Trebizon won't be unhappy. I hope she won't be lonely in that little single room.'

'She won't be lonely!' exclaimed Tish. 'Will she, Mara?'

The two friends had just been along there and peeped into the room through the crack of the door. Ingrid had been sitting in front of the mirror there, applying some night cream and noting with satisfaction that her light golden tan had by no means gone, in spite of the English winter.

She had gazed lovingly at the image in the mirror and the image had gazed lovingly back at her.

'Ingrid will be fine, Mrs Barry,' nodded Mara.

After all, she was now sharing a room with the one she really loved.

It was just before Lights Out. Tish had mysteriously disappeared downstairs. In fact Robbie had turned up at Court

House, thrown some gravel up at a window in the front and asked Jenny to find her.

'What's all the racket about?' asked Rebecca, from her bed. She was lying face down on the pillow and feeling tearful. 'Oh, Mara, I can't get to sleep.'

'You are thinking about Robbie?' Mara whispered from the next bed.

'Yes.'

'You neglected him this term, Rebecca. You know that!'

'I know I have.' Rebecca paused. 'The tennis is getting really important now.' She paused again. 'Oh, Mara, isn't it difficult?'

Tish came back into the room and put a note under Rebecca's pillow. 'From Robbie,' she said. She was holding something else, behind her back.

'Oh, and he also asked me to say what kind of a girl would leave a poor little one-armed bear outside to freeze to death on a night like this.'

She produced Biffy. His battered brown face looked startled, with particles of frost clinging to it, and his clothes had gone as stiff as metal.

'Oh, poor Biffy!' exclaimed Rebecca. She reached her hand out from under the bedclothes and took hold of the frozen bear.

Gently she put him under her pillow. He should have thawed out by the morning.

Maybe he wasn't such a bad bear, after all.

SIXTEEN

LOOKING FORWARD

The arctic weather continued. The last weekend of the term arrived and the hockey pitches were still frozen stiff. Driving conditions throughout most of England were hazardous.

Trebizon would break up the following Thursday and the seven-a-sides tournament was due to take place on the Friday.

At Queensbury Collegiate in Gloucestershire, the Director of Sport called a meeting and took the only decision that was open to him.

'They say there may be a thaw next week, but we can't rely on it,' he said. 'At the moment the pitches aren't even playable and even if they were half the teams wouldn't be able to get here anyway.'

It was decided to telephone round to all the schools involved cancelling the tournament for these holidays and fixing a new date for it to take place in the Easter holidays.

When Miss Willis broke the news to Laura, she was surprised to see that the red-headed girl looked rather joyful for a moment.

Then, looking sad and rather subdued, she said:

'Miss Willis. I – I think I ought to stand down as Head of Games next term. Tish Anderson can take over. She had some good ideas for a sevens squad. They were better than mine.'

Miss Willis herself felt that Laura had made some mistakes. But the system at Trebizon was to give the girls complete responsibility for the teams – total. Usually it worked well.

'You can't,' Miss Willis protested. 'It's unheard of. You were elected to do a job and you've got to do it. In any case, I'm sure Tish herself would never agree. Not after all the hard work you've put in for the sevens this term.'

Miss Willis was right.

'Okay then, Tish,' said Laura, later. 'I'll stay on as Head of Games – but only on one condition. That when we start training again next term we have the people you wanted and not the ones I did.'

'Fine!' said Tish, suddenly very happy. Then she had a thought. 'But what about Joss?'

Laura had already asked Miss Willis about that.

'Well, you know she's coming back for good at Easter? She'll be home a week before the new date they've fixed, so that's okay!'

'Thank goodness!' said Tish.

There was great excitement in Court House when they heard the news.

As for the girls in the other Houses – well they weren't arguing any longer.

'If Laura wants so many from Court House, then it must be okay. She's always fair!'

'They're a lot of Amazons over there anyway,' said a girl in Sterndale, the least sporting of the Houses. 'Who wants to be like them!'

Rebecca settled down to the last few days of term with quiet enjoyment. There was a Christmas party over at Syon House but she decided to avoid it. She thought she'd rather not see Robbie for a while. Perhaps next term.

It was just pleasant, the six of them being together again.

Sue was relieved to be able to bring the violin back into the room sometimes, because there was a hectic amount of practice required for the Christmas concert. Mara would sit poring over her books, for she was studying hard again, with a beatific smile on her face. Rebecca had bought her some earplugs at the chemist shop in the town.

Mara herself sang beautifully in the joint choral production at Garth College – and told them all that the party that was held afterwards was the best ever.

The five friends were very proud of Sue when she was given a long ovation at the Christmas concert, having played two very difficult pieces, perfect at last. She'd already won the House Music Cup that term and was now considered to be a very promising musician.

'But I'm looking forward to getting out of doors and playing some hockey next term,' she told Rebecca. 'I like it in the spring term!'

'So am I,' said Rebecca. 'I won't be playing tennis for the county, that's for sure.' She would have to go back down the ladder after Christmas as an Under-16.

Ingrid departed in the manner in which she'd come. The big Swedish car with the pennant glided to a halt outside Court House on the last morning of term. Hanging out of the front windows of Court House they watched her walk towards the car below, looking as calm and beautiful as ever. She was wearing the very same arresting blue outfit that she'd arrived in, and her hands were inside her big white fur muff.

Her distinguished-looking father shook hands with Mrs Barrington. They were returning to Sweden now, in time for Christmas.

'Have you enjoyed it here, Ingrid?' asked the house-mistress. 'Do you think we've helped you to improve your English?'

'I have enjoyed it very much, thank you,' replied Ingrid with a dignified nod. 'It has been most interesting. My English, also, is much improved.'

There was no crunch of frost as the car drove away. The thaw had arrived, after all.

Later that day Rebecca's coach took her past the rolling grounds of Queensbury Collegiate, just before it reached the town where her grandmother lived.

It was going to be such fun, coming up here in the Easter holidays and playing in the seven-a-sides. There'd be Tish, Sue, Aba, Jenny – and Laura and Eleanor and Sheila and Wanda! And Joss of course. It would be marvellous to have Joss back! Would she have changed after a year in the States?

'All the daffodils will be out when we come!' thought Rebecca, gazing at the acres of green playing fields, with forest beyond. 'They have masses and masses of daffodils here in the spring. Gran can come for the day and watch – she can meet some of my friends, at last!'

Rebecca smiled. Tish was saying that they were going to win the tournament – that was Tish all over. But at least it was going to be fun trying!

'Yes, I'm sure Gran will want to come,' she decided.

JELLYBEAN
Tessa Duder

A sensitive modern novel about Geraldine, alias 'Jellybean', who leads a rather solitary life as the only child of a single parent. She's tired of having to fit in with her mother's busy schedule, but a new friend and a performance of 'The Nutcracker Suite' change everything.

THE PRIESTS OF FERRIS
Maurice Gee

Susan Ferris and her cousin Nick return to the world of O which they had saved from the evil Halfmen, only to find that O is now ruled by cruel and ruthless priests. Can they save the inhabitants of O from tyranny? An action-packed and gripping story by the author of prize-winning THE HALFMEN OF O.

THE SEA IS SINGING
Rosalind Kerven

In her seaside Shetland home, Tess is torn between the plight of the whales and loyalty to her father and his job on the oil rig. A haunting and thought-provoking novel.

BACK HOME
Michelle Magorian

A marvellously gripping story of an irrepressible girl's struggle to adjust to a new life. Twelve-year-old Rusty, who had been evacuated to the United States when she was seven, returns to the grey austerity of post-war Britain.

THE BEAST MASTER
Andre Norton

Spine-chilling science fiction – treachery and revenge! Hosteen Storm is a man with a mission to find and punish Brad Quade, the man who killed his father long ago on Terra, the planet where life no longer exists.

THE PRIME MINISTER'S BRAIN
Gillian Cross

The fiendish DEMON HEADMASTER plans to gain control of No. 10 Downing Street and lure the Prime Minister into his evil clutches.

JASON BODGER AND THE PRIORY GHOST
Gene Kemp

A ghost story, both funny and exciting, about Jason, the bane of every teacher's life, who is pursued by the ghost of a little nun from the twelfth century!

HALFWAY ACROSS THE GALAXY AND TURN LEFT
Robin Klein

A humorous account of what happens to a family banished from their planet Zygron, when they have to spend a period of exile on Earth.

SUPER GRAN TO THE RESCUE
Forrest Wilson

The punchpacking, baddiebiffing escapades of the world's No. 1 senior citizen superhero – Super Gran! Now a devastating series on ITV!

TOM TIDDLER'S GROUND
John Rowe Townsend

Vic and Brain are given an old rowing boat which leads to the unravelling of a mystery and a happy reunion of two friends. An exciting adventure story.

THE FINDING
Nina Bawden

Alex doesn't know his birthday because he was found abandoned next to Cleopatra's Needle, so instead of a birthday he celebrates his Finding. After inheriting an unexpected fortune, Alex's life suddenly becomes very exciting indeed.

RACSO AND THE RATS OF NIMH
Jane Leslie Conly

When fieldmouse Timothy Frisby rescues young Racso, the city rat, from drowning it's the beginning of a friendship and an adventure, The two are caught up in the struggle of the Rats of NIMH to save their home from destruction. A powerful sequel to MRS FRISBY AND THE RATS OF NIMH.

NICOBOBINUS
Terry Jones

Nicobobinus and his friend, Rosie, find themselves in all sorts of intriguing adventures when they set out to find the Land of the Dragons long ago. Stunningly illustrated by Michael Foreman.

FRYING AS USUAL
Joan Lingard

When Mr Francetti breaks his leg it looks as if his fish restaurant will have to close so Toni, Rosita and Paula decide to keep things going.

DRIFT
William Mayne

A thrilling adventure of a young boy and an Indian girl, stranded on a frozen floating island in the North American wilderness.

COME SING, JIMMY JO
Katherine Paterson

An absorbing story about eleven-year-old Jimmy Jo's rise to stardom, and the problem of coping with fame.